Sea Girls

Return to Fortuna

Sea Girls

Return to Fortuna

g.g. elliot

Piccadilly Press • London

First published in Great Britain in 2007
by Piccadilly Press Ltd,
5 Castle Road, London NW1 8PR
www.piccadillypress.co.uk

A catalogue record for this book is available from the British Library

ISBN: 978 1 85340 917 2 (trade paperback)

1 3 5 7 9 10 8 6 4 2

Printed in the UK by CPI Bookmarque, Croydon, CR0 4TD
Typeset by Carolyn Griffiths, Cambridge
Set in ACaslon and Present

Cover design by Simon Davis
Illustration by Sue Hellard

Papers used by Piccadilly Press are produced from
forests grown and managed as a renewable resource,
and which conform to the requirements of recognised forestry
accreditation schemes.

Chapter 1

IT WOULD HAVE BEEN a very strange sight indeed, had anyone been around to witness it. Picture a warm, sunny day in early autumn. Suddenly, in the middle of the English Channel, three heads pop up above the surface of the water. Three heads belonging to three teenage girls, who had just escaped from a strange subterranean world miles beneath the sea's surface. One of the girls, Lydia, had never been above the water before and blinked at the sky stretching over her in pure wonder. Meanwhile, Polly and Lisa looked around until they spotted, far on the horizon, a dark line that they hoped and prayed was England. The three girls, all superb swimmers like the rest of their race, headed towards land.

A few hours had passed when they finally reached the

deserted beach and flopped, exhausted, on to the soft, yellow sand in the late afternoon sun. For Polly and Lisa it was a huge relief to be on land again after their recent nightmare, but Lydia simply could not stop staring at the blue sky and the white billowing clouds. How could anything be so beautiful?

'Any idea where we are, Poll?' asked Lisa after a few minutes.

Polly looked around again. 'Sort of. I'm pretty sure I've been here before but I can't quite place it. A lot of these beaches look the same to me.'

'Are they all as incredible as this?' asked Lydia, her sea-green eyes wide with wonder.

Polly didn't answer, suddenly feeling a sense of urgency. 'I think we should walk round the headland and see if we can find any sign of life before the sun goes down, or at least someone we can ask about where we are. Do you think anyone will still be looking for us, Lisa?'

Two months before, Polly and Lisa had disappeared from the surface. At that point, the girls, who had recently discovered they could breathe naturally under-water, had been trying to show this to their new friend Matt. They had dived deep into the sea and had been sucked into a cave, which led to a lower ocean.

Lisa laughed. 'You've got to be joking! They must think we drowned by now.'

The three girls strolled along the damp foreshore.

Although the sun was about to dip behind the cliffs, they were not the least bit cold. Not only did their race not feel the cold as much as other people, but they were still wearing their amazing fast-dry swimming costumes from the underwater city.

After a few minutes, they came across a rocky promontory that jutted out almost to the sea. When they'd rounded the headland, a small town came into view, tucked behind a little harbour with a few fishing boats bobbing on the water. Along the curved beach leading to the harbour was a group of surfers packing up to go home for the day. Lisa, rather typically, left the other two and walked straight up to them.

"Scuse me!' she said, trying to sound as casual as possible. 'Me and my mates are a bit lost. Can you tell us where we are exactly?'

The boys stared at the tall, fit-looking girls in their figure-hugging suits. Their blond hair and green eyes made them all look like sisters. A couple of them thought there was something familiar about Lisa, but neither could place where they'd seen her before.

One of the boys, who looked slightly older than the others, spoke up. 'This is Maplesea. Where've you guys come from? We didn't see any boats come into the harbour.'

'We swam here,' said Polly, who had just joined Lisa. Lydia stood a little behind the girls, looking slightly wary of the strangers.

The boy looked up at the tall cliffs enclosing the bay. 'Where from exactly? There's nowhere you can reach the beach from for miles in either direction. That's why we use this place.'

Polly and Lisa glanced at each other, and Lisa quickly changed the subject. 'Waves been any good today?' she asked.

Luckily the boy let his question go unanswered. 'Nah, rubbish. Wind's all wrong. We've just been up at the north coast. A few guys just got back from the World Surf Championships in Sydney and were holding a sort of workshop.'

Polly grabbed Lisa's hand tightly. They both knew exactly what the other was thinking.

'Who was there, exactly?' Polly asked, as casually as she could muster. 'We know a few of the top surfers, used to hang out with them . . .'

'There was Sean Harrison, Brendan McLean, Billy Jackson, oh yeah and Matt Miller – he turned up a bit later.'

Polly tried to conceal her excitement at hearing Matt's name.

'Oh right, how was he?'

'He was OK, considering . . . Poor bloke's been a bit crap since . . . well, you must know.'

Polly and Lisa knew all right.

'Since what?' Polly asked, trying to sound innocent.

'Since those girls disappeared.'

'Disappeared?' Lisa repeated excitedly, trying hard not to squeak. 'Are they dead? Did they find the bodies?'

Polly tried to hide a smile behind her hand.

The boys looked at them strangely again. The report of the two girls who had simply disappeared at sea had been the biggest story for ages in the West Country. No trace of them had ever been found.

''Course not,' the boy replied. 'They probably sank without trace. Fish food, I reckon. We all think Miller was lucky not to get banged up. Nobody knows what really happened except him. He says they just dived over the side of his boat and disappeared. The cops gave us a real hard time too. They spoke to all of us surfers. C'mon, you must have read about it – it was all over the papers.'

''Course we did, it's just that we've been away and forgot,' said Lisa. 'We're actually friends of his, but we haven't seen him for ages. Hey, have any of you got a mobile we could borrow, just for a second? I'd really like to give him a quick ring. He might even come down and see us, when he knows we're back.'

The lads looked impressed but slightly puzzled. Matt Miller was still a god in the surfing world, despite his recent form and despite the cloud hanging over him. Most people knew he would never knowingly have harmed a fly but, gossip being gossip, he was still talked about with deep suspicion.

As the boy passed Lisa his phone, Lydia tried to take in what they were saying. She was continually distracted, however, as her eyes roamed to the road along the seafront where cars – which she had never seen before – were passing by. Where she came from people travelled only by boats on canals – or by swimming. There weren't any proper roads in Fortuna.

Lisa couldn't believe her luck when one of the boys said he had Matt's number stored. It was fantastic to hear his voice when he answered, 'Hello?'

'Matt, don't freak out but it's me – Lisa. Remember? I'm with Polly. We're safe, and at a place called Maplesea.'

There was a short hesitation and then Matt's familiar voice came back on the line. 'Is this some kind of a sicko joke? I thought you people had had enough of that by now. Who are you and who put you up to it? If this is a wind-up, I hope you think it's funny, 'cos I don't.'

He sounded ready to hang up, so Lisa quickly interjected. 'Hey, calm down. Look, it is me, honest. Hang on a sec. I think I can prove it. I'll call you right back.'

Polly asked the boy whose phone it was to take a picture of her and Lisa, then sent it to Matt's phone.

He rang back almost immediately.

'Where the hell have you been?' he asked in a strained voice, as if he had just seen a ghost. 'Do you have *any* idea what I've gone through recently? I've been practically accused of murdering you two.'

Lisa glanced at Polly, who was trying to put her ear to the phone too. 'Look, I can't go into it now, but there is an explanation, I promise. All we can say is that we're really sorry about what you've been through and that what happened to us was more weird than anything you can possibly imagine. You'll understand when we see you again.' She dropped her voice. 'Is there any chance you could come and get us? We're completely stranded. We've literally only just got back. Oh yeah, and we've brought someone with us.'

The voice that responded was loud and angry. 'Back? Back? Where on earth from?' Matt was silent for a second and then his voice softened. 'Look, enough of this. Where did you say you were?'

'We're on the beach at Maplesea. Do you know it?'

'Yeah, quite well. My mates do a bit of surfing there.'

'We're with a few of them now. I'm using one of their phones. We could wait here for you on the beach. We'll probably be the only people here.'

'Fine, I'm not that far away. I'll leave now and should be with you in about an hour.'

The surfers had caught snatches of the girl's conversation and were beginning to wonder what was

7

going on. Luckily, as there were three girls there, they didn't make the connection with the two missing girls they'd heard about. Lisa gave the boy back his phone and they said their goodbyes to the strangely-dressed girls, picked up their boards and sauntered off to their ancient camper-van, parked up on the roadside.

Just as the light was fading, the familiar figure of Matt Miller, with his shock of sun-bleached hair and motor-bike gear, appeared. When he saw Polly and Lisa, he hesitated for a few seconds and then ran headlong towards them, kicking up the sand in his wake. By the time he reached them, all of his anger had vanished and he hugged the two girls as if they had been his very own family. Tears of relief were streaming down his tanned face. Lydia could only sit and watch in fascination. Touched as she was by the reunion, she couldn't take her eyes off the new arrival . . . there was something so familiar about him.

Eventually, when the three friends had stopped hug-ging each other, Matt cast his eye over to Lydia. As he examined her face, he felt the same fascination. Polly and Lisa caught their expressions and smiled. Both wondered if Lydia and Matt might fancy each other. After all Lydia was very beautiful and just about every girl in the world fancied Matt.

Lisa spoke first, hesitantly. 'Lydia, this is Matt – he's

a friend of ours.' Matt put his hand out to shake hers. Lydia looked slightly confused at his outstretched palm; it was a greeting unknown in Fortuna.

Polly broke in. 'She's from where we've just come from, Matt: Fortuna. It's an underwater city. We only got back this afternoon, and you're the first friend we've seen. We haven't even spoken to our mums and dads yet. They still don't know we're alive. While we're phoning them Lydia can try to explain about everything, or at least make a start. I'm sorry, but can we use *your* phone now?'

Like Matt, Polly and Lisa's parents could hardly believe what they were hearing and could barely speak, they were so overcome with emotion. The only difference was that they recognised their adopted daughters' voices instantly. Polly's parents, who lived only about twenty miles away, told them they were driving over to pick them up at once and said they'd arrange for Lisa's parents to come over to their place straight away, too. When they asked her where she'd been, Polly said that she would explain everything when she saw them again.

Quarter of an hour later, when the girls came back to Matt and Lydia, Matt's mouth was hanging open in disbelief. 'Is this all true, what she's saying?' he managed to get out. 'It sounds as if you've all taken crazy pills.'

'How far have you got?' Polly asked Lydia.

'I was just telling him how I met you two,' Lydia said quietly. 'But I haven't begun to tell him how you ended up in Fortuna.'

Matt turned to Polly and Lisa. 'This is completely mad. A land under the sea? You've got to be kidding, haven't you?'

'It's all true,' said Lisa. 'Ever since we last saw you we've been more or less prisoners in Fortuna. It's where we all originally came from – where everyone with that fish symbol was born. You too! We were taken up to the surface because our lives were in danger – our parents weren't allowed to have babies. We were left on the beach in the hope that someone would find us and look after us.'

Matt was quiet for a short while and then said in a faraway voice, 'You, Polly, me . . . and Kelly, maybe!'

'Who's Kelly?' Polly and Lisa said in chorus.

'While you were away, a girl called Kelly phoned me. She'd read in the papers about you two disappearing. She said she could breathe underwater and everything. So can I, by the way – she showed me.'

'Weren't *we* supposed to show you how to do that?' said Lisa and she and Polly laughed for the first time in ages.

'Glad you think that's funny,' said Matt. 'The police sure didn't.'

'Did it get on telly?' asked Polly.

'You don't know the half of it. It was everywhere – on

the telly, the radio, in the papers, you name it. And I was accused of killing you at first.'

Polly and Lisa looked at each other and tried hard to take it in. It seemed very strange to hear stories about themselves being murdered.

'Look,' Matt continued, 'there is someone who believed my story. His name's Chris Buckley and he's a professor at Cambridge. He'll really want to meet you three, and I bet he'll know what to do next.'

Matt took the girls to a café on the harbourfront for a quick cup of tea, which Lydia found quite the oddest drink she had ever tasted. As he watched her drink it, Matt still couldn't work out what he found quite so fascinating about her.

Chapter 2

POLLY'S PARENTS WERE ECSTATIC to see Polly and Lisa. Their strange outfits and the surprising presence of Matt Miller and another girl didn't even register with them as Polly's mother broke into instant tears and hugged her adopted daughter, then Lisa, so hard it took their breath away.

Polly introduced her parents to her new friends, Matt and Lydia, then the three girls bundled into the back of the car to drive home, Matt following behind on his motorbike. When they got back, the girls decided not to start their story until Lisa's parents' arrival, which was expected to be within half an hour. While they were waiting, Polly took Lisa and Lydia up to her room, where she tried to sort them out with more suitable clothes.

Lydia's head was reeling. The journey in the car had

been extraordinary. For a start, having lived in a relatively small dome, she could hardly comprehend the distance they had just travelled, let alone the idea that the journey was just a fraction of the size of England and that England was just a small part of the whole surface of the world. She thought the car was an incredible machine and marvelled at the number of other vehicles they passed on the road and how different everyone looked from each other. Most people in Fortuna had green eyes and straight blond hair – as she, Polly, Lisa and Matt did. She also found it difficult to get into her head that most of the population in this part of the world had their own homes. Back in Fortuna they all lived communally.

Now she had to put on jeans and a T-shirt – items she had never seen before. Lydia, who was not used to laughing, thought bras were the oddest items of clothing she had ever come across and giggled at the idea of wearing one herself.

When the doorbell rang, Lisa rushed downstairs to meet her parents. They laughed and cried with joy as they saw each other, and Lisa realised that despite all the adventures she'd undergone in Fortuna, she'd missed them with all her heart.

When they were settled in the living room, Polly began their story. She started with the discovery, all those months earlier, of the little fish symbol on her back, lifting up the back of her jumper to show them. Then she told them about how she discovered she could breathe underwater.

Polly went on to remind the two sets of parents how she had met Lisa at a swimming competition and explained how she had noticed an identical symbol on Lisa's back. They had immediately connected, she said, in a way that neither of them had connected with anyone else before. As they had got to know each other they discovered they had both been adopted and even more peculiarly, had both been found, abandoned, on a beach. It turned out, she said, that Lisa too could breathe underwater. Then she described how they had both gone to the surf championships and saw that the winner, Matt, also had the tiny fish mark in the same place on his back and how it turned out that he, like them, had been abandoned as a baby.

'We began to realise there was something very weird about us all,' she said. 'Something connected with water. Matt didn't believe us at first . . .' She began to giggle. 'But I think he does now.'

'So what happened then?' asked Polly's father, shaking his head in disbelief.

'We decided to prove to Matt that we really could breathe underwater. We got Matt to take us out in his dad's boat. Then we dived as deep as we could and were exploring the rocks and caves down there. We were down for quite a while and were about to swim back up to the surface when it happened.'

Lisa took over. 'I saw these fish, you see, going into a cave, and I swam up to them. Before I knew what was happening, I was being sucked in and through a gap in the rocks – there was nothing I could do because the current pulling me was so strong. Polly came to see what had happened to me and got sucked in too. We found ourselves in a lower ocean.'

'Lower ocean?' the adults asked.

'Under the seabed there is another vast ocean, lit by a faint light and full of weird creatures. We were scared stiff.'

The two sets of parents looked at each other across the room. They didn't know what to think. Underwater breathing . . . lower oceans . . . Were their daughters making this up to cover what they had really been up to?

Polly continued. 'This bit's going to be even more difficult to believe. We were trying to find a way back through the rocks when this enormous thing, shaped like a huge fish, came up to us. Before we could do anything, its jaws opened and we were swallowed up.'

'It turned out to be a kind of submarine,' said Lisa, 'driven by a couple of blokes in strange outfits – a bit like the ones we were wearing when we came back. They took us downwards for ages until we eventually came to this enormous dome under the sea.' She looked at the unbelieving faces around her. 'Look, I know it sounds crazy.'

Lydia, seeing that her friend was struggling, then spoke for the first time. 'Inside the dome is a land called Fortuna. It is where I have lived all my life.'

She continued by telling them briefly how Fortuna had come about – that the city had sunk beneath the waves many centuries earlier. She described this amazing land within the crystal globe, how it was powered by harnessing the heat from the earth's core and how daytime and night-time were simulated by huge generators that turned the lights on in the morning and off at night. She then told them how it was ruled by an evil regime headed by the wicked governor Solon and his army of Polizia, who kept hundreds of slaves in an underground prison called Devilla. She told them how, in order to control the population, anyone who wasn't part of Solon's family was compulsorily terminated at sixty. And not everyone was allowed to have children.

'We were taken straight to this guy Solon,' Lisa broke in, 'and though it didn't seem so bad at first, we realised we were virtually imprisoned in this flash apartment, and this other guy, Petruvio, was there to guard us.'

All three girls talked and talked about the beautiful but bizarre city, with its multi-levelled waterways and towering classical buildings, but they were well aware that they could never do it justice. Their audience was finding it almost impossible to take in.

The most difficult part came when Polly and Lisa had to tell their adoptive parents that it was Fortuna where they had all been born and that there was a chance that their real parents were still alive there.

'As Lydia said, not everyone is allowed to have children,' said Lisa, 'and those who are, are only permitted to have one. We must have been forbidden babies. As such, our lives were in danger. There was one person, called Maricia, who tried to save the babies. She knew a way to the surface and she arranged for us to be taken up and left on the land – that's where we were found.'

By the time they had all finished, their audience was stunned into complete silence. The story was so fantastic that nobody but a science fiction writer could have made it up. Indeed, if the girls had decided to lie about where they had been, their parents had to admit that there were far more believable stories they could have come up with. Perhaps it was true after all . . .

Later that evening, Matt rang Chris Buckley, the Cambridge professor who, over the past couple of months, had become his friend and confidant. It was past midnight but Chris Buckley only had to hear the tone of the surfer's voice to realise he had something important to say. Half an hour later, the professor, who hadn't interrupted or even asked one single question, simply said he would join them as soon as possible.

The young historian could hardly think straight. He knew that this incredible development had to be the culmination of all he had worked for and that for him it was by far the most important thing that had ever happened. The idea that the girls were still alive and had been trapped under the sea in a strange under-water world was almost too much for his mind to take in.

Chris Buckley hardly slept and set off from Cambridge as soon as it was light, arriving at Polly's house just after breakfast. When Matt had introduced him to everyone and when he had been filled in on all the things that Matt had omitted over the phone, he asked if he might join the conversation regarding what they should do next.

Polly's father was the first to speak. 'We are going to have to tell the newspapers that Polly and Lisa have been found. They're bound to find out sooner or later, and much better if they hear it from us first.'

'Do you realise what that would mean?' asked the professor. 'If we tell them the truth it would be the biggest story in the history of the press. I wonder if we have to tell them exactly where they've been?'

Polly's father rubbed his chin. 'They have to have

been somewhere. What could they reasonably have been doing?'

Matt spoke up. 'They could have been with a load of surfers. We spend the whole summer hanging out on beaches, sleeping in vans, beach huts, park shelters – you name it. Don't worry. I can give you a whole bunch of names, if you want. My mates are cool, as long as they know they're not going to get into any deep . . . er, *trouble*, they'll say practically anything you want.'

'It wouldn't do much for our daughters' reputations,' Polly's mother chipped in rather glibly.

Lisa smiled. She had never really minded what people had thought of her anyway, and rather liked the idea.

'It would give us some breathing space,' said Chris Buckley. 'I do have contacts who are capable of influencing what the press write. If they realise how important this all is, I think they could be persuaded to leave us alone for a bit. How do you girls feel about it? Are you worried about what people might say?'

Polly and Lisa shot each other a glance and shrugged. 'I'd rather get a bad reputation for running away than for telling what people are going to think are huge lies. I don't reckon anyone would believe us,' said Polly.

'What about school?' asked Lisa's father.

'I reckon we'd be heroes if we went back with a story like Matt's,' laughed Lisa, much to the disapproving looks of her mother and father.

Matt suddenly looked slightly worried. 'I haven't rung Kelly yet! Is it OK if she comes round tomorrow? She needs to know what's happened.'

'Who's Kelly?' asked Lisa's mother.

Matt explained about Kelly. 'She's one of us – she was born in Fortuna. She's really great, just like Polly and Lisa.'

The two friends glanced at each other and realised they were both going red.

Lydia then spoke, quietly but forcefully. 'Before I left there had been a lot of talk about the threat from Solon. He was planning to attack the part of Fortuna where I was brought up. It's called the Southern Quarter. Theron, our leader, had decided that there was to be a huge rebellion. It was either that or be terminated by Solon's Polizia. I promised the people of the Southern Quarter that I'd do anything I could to help them. I will have to go back before long. Polly and Lisa are not under any obligation, but I'm afraid I am.'

'I'm not sure about that,' said Lisa. 'If it wasn't for the people of the Southern Quarter, we'd either be dead or in Devilla, the slave prison. I must admit the idea of going back feels pretty ghastly though. I certainly don't want to see Solon or Petruvio ever again. But anyway, how could anyone possibly get back down to Fortuna?'

'Silas, the old fisherman, told me he would return to the gap every thirty days and wait.'

'I'm sorry,' said Lisa's father, to the girls, 'but you can't be serious about going back. If the situation down there is as dangerous as you say, you'd be mad. I just can't allow it.'

Later the next day, Matt got a phonecall from Kelly to tell him that she had just arrived at the local station and needed picking up. He set off at once to give her a lift to Polly's house.

As soon as she stepped inside, Kelly found herself instantly and rather uncannily at home with Polly and Lisa, though she felt rather overwhelmed by Lydia – Matt had explained the situation as best he could on the phone earlier.

The five of them spent the afternoon catching up and discussing Fortuna with the professor, revelling in this longed-for opportunity to share their innermost thoughts and experiences.

Chapter 3

F OR LYDIA, THE NEXT few days were to be quite extraordinary. Wherever she turned, she encountered things that she could hardly have believed possible and most of them had to be explained to her in detail. However much Polly and Lisa had tried to prepare her for life on the surface, nothing could match up to what she actually saw with her own eyes.

From the moment she first encountered television, she could hardly be dragged away from it. She couldn't figure out how it worked or how all the people who appeared got in there. Many of the reality shows, especially the one where celebrities were made to suffer all sorts of indignities in a jungle, caused her to wonder what sort of a crazy society she had come to. The wildlife programmes were even more puzzling. It seemed almost incomprehensible to someone who had come from a land where only rats and cockroaches had survived that such a vast array of bizarre creatures could share the planet with human beings. Elephants, in particular, fascinated her and Matt promised he would take her to see some as soon as was possible.

Polly's parents' house was rather small, so Matt asked Lydia if she'd like to come and stay at his place for a while. At first Polly and Lisa felt rather jealous, but they realised all the same it was probably the best solution for the foreseeable future – Matt and Lydia had become practically inseparable. Not in a boyfriend/girlfriend kind of way perhaps, but they seemed extremely happy and relaxed in each other's company.

Matt decided he would explain everything to his parents as soon as they met Lydia. For the time being, however, he told them that she was a surfer groupie he had met on his travels who had just arrived from abroad with nowhere to stay. This was not unusual, so they thought little of it.

The first journey Lydia had taken in a car had been in the dark, so the next, in Matt's father's huge 4x4, left her just as astonished, and she spent most of it with her nose pressed against the window. She could hardly take in the vast panoramas in every direction, or the hundreds of cars, lorries and motorbikes that flashed past. When she saw a plane passing overhead she was lost for words.

The little towns and villages they drove through were also completely unlike anything she had ever witnessed. And then there were all the different kinds of people – some with dark hair, some with light hair, some pale-skinned and others almost coal black – all seeming to live together in harmony. She was dying to ask questions but realised how strange they'd sound until Matt had told his parents the real story.

At one point, as they were driving, Matt's father asked if she'd like to listen to the radio. She didn't know what a radio was, so when he turned on the news, the poor girl looked momentarily round the interior of their car to see where the extra voice was coming from.

Thanks to his father's boat building business, Matt's adoptive parents were quite wealthy and lived in a large detached house with several acres of garden, a swimming pool and a tennis court. Lydia's room, which Matt's mother had quickly prepared, was large and airy, with its own bathroom, dressing room and, best of all, television. Lydia had been frightened almost out of her wits on her arrival at Matt's house when the family's huge Great Dane, Shrek, had run up to her to greet her. She simply had no idea what dogs were, or cats for that matter, or the horse in the paddock outside or the cows and sheep in the fields beyond. When she had first seen Matt's little sister on her horse, Lydia had thought it very funny, as if it was some kind of stunt for her entertainment. When she was told that the cows and sheep were eaten by humans, she couldn't believe that people who appeared to be so nice would do such things and was revolted. For many centuries, Fortunans had been mostly vegetarian, apart from eating fish and, in the Southern Quarter, rats. The inhabitants had killed or eaten all their own animals shortly after the floods had caused the city to be enclosed.

It was on the second day of her stay with Matt that their relationship became clearer. She was talking about the other babies that had been brought to the surface.

'Do we know how many there were?' Matt asked her.

'All in all, about twenty-five.'

'So there are still twenty or so out there who don't know . . .'

'The only thing we know about them is their numbers.'

'Numbers?' asked Matt, confused.

Lydia realised that though she, Lisa and Polly had filled Matt in on most of the important facts about the Southern Quarter and Maricia, the old lady who had organised for the babies to come to the surface, no mention had been made of the numbering system designed to identify them should there ever be a time when they'd be reacquainted with their parents.

25

'You know the little fish mark on your back? Well, it's got a number hidden in it. You can only see it with a special viewer.'

'Yeah. I heard about that. I was away when Kelly went to have hers examined.'

'Have you got anything we could look at it through?'

Matt hesitated. 'My dad's got this incredibly powerful magnifying glass on a stand which he uses to draw up sea-charts. I'll just go and get it – it's in his office.'

When he returned, he lifted his T-shirt and asked Lydia to try to read it. Lydia stared through the contraption, trying to focus. Eventually it became clear. When she stood up suddenly, her face was as pale as if she'd seen a ghost.

Matt caught her strange expression. 'What's up? What did you see?'

Lydia struggled for words. 'I – I saw the number . . .' she stuttered. 'It's fourteen.'

'So? What's so special about fourteen?'

Lydia looked straight into Matt's eyes as everything gradually became clear. 'It's the number of my brother. I knew there was something special about you.'

'Your *brother*?'

'My twin brother.'

They both sat and stared at one another, open mouthed, and then Lydia burst into a mixture of laughter and tears. 'Don't you see? That's why we have become so close!'

Matt nodded slowly. 'We've got the same parents!'

It was decided for the time being that Polly and Lisa wouldn't contact any of their friends until they knew exactly what cover story they'd use and had decided on a course of action. This was far more difficult than they first realised and it became almost impossible to go out for fear of being seen. Polly and Lisa found it hard enough to adjust to life back in England without this additional restriction on their freedom. All they could do was meet secretly at each other's houses. They soon realised that they couldn't go on like this for long and that something had to be resolved. When they next met up with Matt, Kelly and Lydia, however, the conversation soon turned to Fortuna, Devilla and the wickedness of Solon's regime.

'Has anyone got any idea what Devilla is really like?' asked Kelly.

Lydia looked very serious as she began to explain. She described to them the huge underground prison from which few had ever escaped. The poor captives, she told them, were brought outside every night to man the factories or work in the fields. Many were brought into the city to do all the work that the Fortunans weren't prepared to do. They left by the time the

Fortunans awoke and so were never seen.

'We saw them coming back from their work once,' said Lisa. 'They looked completely exhausted.'

Polly sounded upset. 'It was as if all the spirit had been sucked out of them. It was so awful. I'll never forget it.'

'How can the people of Fortuna allow it?' asked Kelly.

Lydia shrugged, telling the little group that most of the Fortunans acted like they knew nothing about it – which might have been true since they were really too scared to ask questions. Solon's spies were everywhere and it was not unusual for people who questioned what was happening to simply disappear without trace. Indeed it was thought by some that they ended up in the very place they were asking about – Devilla. Even children were beaten if they asked too many questions.

Matt wondered if this terrible state of affairs was all down to Solon, but his sister told him that Solon was just the latest in a long line of tyrants and that the Polizia were believed to take their orders from him. There were two types, she said: those that acted as armed police and those that operated in secret. These were the ones that were most dangerous.

After they had been at their respective homes a week or so, and despite their many discussions, they decided that they all had to get together with the express purpose of working out what they were to do next – if anything. Polly and Lisa realised that Lydia would want to go back to Fortuna soon and if she did, that might be the last they'd see of her. The more they thought of the poor people of Devilla, however, and the more they realised that their real parents could well be there, the nagging idea began to enter their heads that perhaps they ought to go too. This finally became clear in a conversation over the phone late one night.

Lisa breathed in deeply and broached the subject. 'I was talking to Lydia last night. She says she wants to go back soon. She says she's feeling homesick and that her place is with her people, especially if the rebellion is about to happen.'

'I know,' replied Polly. 'I spoke to her about half an hour ago. She said that Matt's insisting on going with her now he's discovered she's his twin. I still can't believe it – I knew there was something weird about those two.'

When Polly and Lisa had first heard that Matt and Lydia were brother and sister, they had both taken it in their stride. It seemed to answer all their questions about their closeness and they *did* have a certain resemblance, particularly in the way they moved.

'Do you think he's crazy to want to go to Fortuna?'

Polly hesitated. 'I would have done if he'd said he

wanted to when we first got back but now he's heard all about it from Lydia I'm not so sure. I'm terrified of returning, but I can't bear to think of my real parents suffering down there because of me.'

'I feel even more strongly than that. I feel it's sort of my fault they were sent to Devilla.'

'You couldn't help being born,' reasoned Polly.

'I just feel I ought to do anything I can to help them.'

Polly lowered her voice, worried her parents might overhear the conversation. 'You realise you might never get back.'

'Yeah,' said Lisa, 'but if I stay here I'll always have it on my mind, won't I? I don't think life here can ever be the same again.'

'Your mum and dad would go mad if you go back,' Polly murmured.

Lisa sighed. 'And then some. If I told them I was even thinking about it they'd go ballistic. '

'I think you must be a bit crazy to even consider it. What if you, Matt and Lydia end up in Devilla?'

Lisa sighed. 'I know. And what use would I be in a rebellion?'

They were both silent for a long while.

'Despite all that, I have to go,' said Lisa, with a strange laugh.

'Lisa, you can't leave me here. What would I do without you?'

'Look, Polly, it's not really a decision. I don't think I've got a choice.'

'But your real parents might not even be there, even if you did manage to get into Devilla to look for them.'

'Then we will have tried and failed, but at least we'll have tried.'

'What do you think Kelly wants to do?' Polly asked.

'I know she's really keen to find her real parents too, but her adoptive mum's quite ill at the moment and she doesn't want to leave her. I don't think she's that scared of the idea, but I reckon it must be easier to be brave if you haven't been there before.'

'So what should *we* do?'

Lisa was silent for a second. 'I reckon we've all got to get together. We can't carry on going back and forth on this – it'll drive us mad.'

'You're right. I'll ring Matt and see what we can fix up.'

A few days later they were all sitting round the pool in Matt's parents' spacious conservatory.

'So,' Lisa began. 'How do we all feel now we've had a chance to think it over? She looked at Matt. 'Are you and Lydia still up for going?'

Lydia spoke quietly. 'As I said before, I know I have no choice. They are my people and I have a duty – it's as simple as that. But I would still completely understand if you said you didn't want to come. It will be very dangerous. So dangerous you might never get back.'

Kelly, who up until that moment had said little, cleared her throat. 'I stayed over here with Matt and Lydia last night, and she told me much more about Fortuna and what she plans to do when she gets back there. I really do want to come, honest, but I just can't leave my mum – my adoptive mum that is. It's a really difficult decision for me because I've always known I was different – right from when I was little. Going to Fortuna would have helped me come to terms with who I really am. But I can't. Do you know what I mean, guys?'

'You bet,' broke in Matt. 'But I feel like there's not really a choice in this for me.'

Lisa suddenly looked very serious. 'Whatever we think about going back, we certainly won't be able to convince our parents, will we? I reckon we're just going to have to do a runner or they'll do their best to stop us going.'

'When would you go?' asked Polly, looking round the little group one at a time. She had been so scared in Fortuna that she hadn't even considered going with them.

'If it were down to just me,' said Lydia, 'though I do want to see so much more of your world, I'd like to go at the first opportunity. I have the feeling that this is going to be the most important period in the history of Fortuna. If its future is going to be decided, I just have to be there.'

She turned to look at Matt. 'Anyway, I have found what I was looking for – my long lost twin – and he already means so much to me. I told you before that Silas, the fisherman, arranged to wait at the gap every thirty days from the day we left. I've been counting the days since we got here, and I calculate that he will be there in fourteen days' time. I think we should be there waiting for him. I know I will be – if you will help me, that is.'

Lisa turned to Lydia. 'The longer we hang about, the worse the situation will be in Fortuna.'

Matt grinned. 'And we won't have so long to chicken out.'

'Do you really think you'll be able to make a difference?' asked Polly.

Lydia smiled. 'I really do. We can prove to them with your photographs that there is another world up here. We can take your cameras and take pictures of Devilla so that everyone gets to know what's really going on.'

'What if Silas doesn't show?' asked Polly, still desperate to talk them out of it. 'There's no way you'd be able to find the way back to the top ocean without his help.'

'If Silas says he will do something, he will,' said

Lydia almost defiantly. 'We might have to wait around for a while, but he wouldn't let us down, that much I can promise.'

By the end of the evening, Lisa, Matt and Lydia had all agreed that they must return to Fortuna, and so it was set. In two weeks' time, almost a month from when they'd left Fortuna, the small group of intrepid travellers were to be ready to try to locate the small cave that led to the great ocean below.

The following week turned out to be torture for Polly. She felt completely split between her loyalty to her friends and her loyalty to her parents. On the one hand, she was scared stiff at the idea of going back, and on the other she didn't want to miss out on the adventure. She talked about it endlessly with Lisa, going over and over the reasons she thought it was such a bad idea, until even she realised that she either had to shut up or go. Eight days after the meeting she rang Lisa again.

'I've decided I'm coming. I just can't let you lot go without me.'

'Of course you're coming,' said Lisa, laughing. 'I knew that all the time you kept telling me how mad we were!'

'I'm going to write a long letter to Mum and Dad to try to explain why I'm doing it.'

'I've already written one to mine. I've decided I'll leave it out for them on the day we go, so that they won't have a chance to stop me. By the time they read it, we'll be gone.'

Lisa was silent for a second, then spoke again, softly. 'Seriously, Poll, I'm so glad you're coming. I don't know if I could have managed it without you. Don't be frightened. We'll be OK if we're together.'

Chapter 4

TRYING TO PREPARE FOR a journey in complete secrecy proved almost impossible. All conversations between the friends had to be carried out not just on their mobiles, but well away from their respective homes. It was essential that their parents had no clue as to what they were planning. Polly and Lisa's parents had been so delighted to have their daughters back that they'd have been heartbroken at the idea of them leaving again. As it was, they kept asking tentatively when they felt they might be ready to go back to school, but Polly and Lisa kept putting them off by saying that they wanted a little more time to acclimatise.

Matt managed to locate some small waterproof backpacks from a surfing suppliers and bought one for each of them. For the contents, they agreed to choose things that they wouldn't be able to get in Fortuna that might be of use. The plan was to get back to the Southern Quarter and put themselves at the disposal of Theron, the leader of the rebels. They would take with them hundreds of photographs, as Lydia had suggested, so that everyone would be able to see what the world above was really like.

Matt felt extremely bad about not informing his friend Chris Buckley of their plan. He decided to send him a letter, which would reach him only after they had left, explaining why he was going to Fortuna and apologising for their secrecy. In many ways he felt Chris could have helped them, giving them useful advice on what devices would be most useful below, but in the end he and his friends felt they just couldn't risk it.

The group began to discuss what they could take with them and agreed that although mobile phones wouldn't work so far under the water, cameras and compasses would. They also agreed that they should probably take as many batteries as possible, as there would be no way of recharging them. Matt also suggested underwater torches, and some sort of spray to repel attackers.

Polly mentioned her worries as to whether they would find the cave that pulled them into the lower ocean again, but Matt assured them all that he'd taken a reading on the boat's sat-nav when the girls dived into the water. He wasn't likely to forget the co-ordinates – he'd given them to the police over and over again when Lisa and Polly had disappeared. Matt was going to arrange for a trusted mate to take them out on his boat.

Polly rang Lisa the evening before they were all due to leave their homes to travel to Traders Beach.

'Are you scared, Lisa?'

'Don't even go there, Poll – but I've never been more excited either. I know I must be completely crazy now! How about you?'

'I've always known I was a bit crazy. I'm just glad in a way we both feel we've got no choice. It would be so easy to walk away from all this now and get on with our normal lives. The trouble is, I really think this *is* my life, and I can't seem to avoid it. I'm still trying to write the letter for my mum and dad. It's taken me flipping ages. How do you say to someone who's loved you and looked after you all your life that you are going to risk it to find your real parents? It seems a bit like a humungous kick in the teeth. How about you?'

Lisa hesitated. 'Search me. I wrote a great long letter at first but then I changed it completely. I've now kept it fairly short and to the point. I just told them I love them and I always will, whatever happens. It's just something I have to do and that I'll see them later,' she said. Then she changed the subject to Kelly. 'I'll really

38

miss her. I wish she could come out in the boat and say a proper goodbye to us, but I know it's going to be over-loaded anyway with us lot.'

It was a cold, grey Friday morning when the four friends eventually set out. They had all left their houses as casually as they could, fairly early in the morning. Polly and Lisa said that they were going to school to try to find out what work they had missed so they could be ready when they went back. Matt and Lydia said they were going to meet some surfer friends – which was perfectly normal for Matt.

The assembled company couldn't help noticing, as they sped out of the harbour in the small speedboat, how Craig, Matt's friend, kept staring at them with something like awe. Matt had told him what was going to happen, but he just couldn't take it all in. He still couldn't quite get to grips with the idea of running a group of people he'd never met miles out to some place in the middle of the sea, simply to leave them there. But he had known Matt for most of his life and trusted him implicitly. If his friend, the great Matt Miller, said it was all right, then it was, and that was all there was to it.

When Matt had taken them to the correct position, he handed the boat's controls to his friend and, without another word, rolled over the side and waited for the others to join him in the water. They then waved to Craig, as cheerily as they could muster, and dived straight down into the cold, grey-green depths. Matt had told him what they planned to do and that they could all breathe underwater, but Craig had found this almost impossible to believe. After an hour or so though, Craig realised that they weren't going to re-surface, and he turned the small boat round and headed back to land, completely mystified and feeling strangely guilty.

Chapter 5

IT TOOK THE TRAVELLERS over an hour, swimming backwards and forwards along the rocky seabed, to find the elusive cave through which water hurtled to the lower ocean – the cave that the two girls had found by accident when the whole adventure started. This time it was made easier by the torches that they had decided to take with them. Eventually Polly noticed a slight current pulling her towards a gap in the rocks. She gathered the others, and with great trepidation pointed to the gap. Polly went first, followed by Lisa, then Matt and finally Lydia. One by one, as they approached the hole in the rocks, they lost control as they were sucked into the gap and through what appeared to be a narrow tunnel.

The four friends emerged dizzy and disorientated at the other end, having been rolled over and over countless times as they had plummeted downwards.

When they were free of the exit, Matt stared in wonder at the immense and sinister ceiling of solid rock that extended in every direction above them. Strangely, as Polly and Lisa had discovered before, there was no need for the torches down there as the whole place was lit by a slightly eerie green glow that seemed to emanate from the seaweed that clung to the rocks above and from the strange luminous creatures that drifted past. As they had feared, there was no one there to meet them, so they were forced to hang around the cave's exit, hoping that the fisherman was on his way. Lydia had sworn that Silas would be along some time on the thirtieth day, but they couldn't help wondering if he might have forgotten.

This feeling was worse for the three girls however, as Matt was now so busy staring in awe at the array of the almost supernatural phenomena around them that he scarcely noticed Silas's absence. The weird and wonderful glowing creatures bore little relationship to anything he'd ever seen – many of them had huge bulbous eyes to penetrate the murky water and others had see-through bodies that revealed all their inner workings. The strangest of all possessed long, waving tentacles with what looked like tiny torches on the ends. None of them, large or small, seemed the least bit frightened of the intruders and even brushed up against them as they passed silently by.

After a couple of hours, however, everyone was starting to feel very frightened. They had tried to occupy themselves, swimming about and studying the weird marine life, but the situation was serious. The idea of being trapped below a ceiling of impenetrable rock was too scary to even contemplate. They knew there was a way back, but they had no idea how they would find it.

Just as they were beginning to panic, they felt a faint vibration through the water, followed by an ominous buzzing noise. After a couple of minutes they could just make out a huge, silver, fish-shaped craft, heading towards them out of the gloom. Lydia gasped in excitement, but just as she was preparing to swim out to meet it, she suddenly froze. The others stared at her trying to work out what was wrong. Lydia waved her arms frantically and indicated for them to swim behind a large clump of drifting seaweed. It wasn't Silas, but another fishing boat passing by. Luckily the searchlight that was scouring the depths in front of the huge craft failed to catch the four friends as they swam frantically for cover. The deafening rumble of the engines as it went past took their breath away.

They stayed where they were until the sinister machine disappeared into the gloom, realising with horror what a disaster it would have been if it had been manned by Solon's men and they had swum out to meet it by mistake.

An hour later, a similar boat loomed into view and drifted to a halt just short of the gap in the rocks. Through the little window in the front, Lydia could just make out the familiar face of Silas. As the friends emerged with utter relief from behind the dark foliage, the huge jaws began to cantilever open, much to the horror of Matt who, despite having heard this process described in detail, had never actually witnessed anything like it. Before they knew what was happening, they were all being sucked in as if being swallowed alive. Polly and Lisa later admitted that they were almost as terrified as they had been the first time.

The two girls hugged each other rapturously, however, when they recognised Silas's stern but kind face through the glass observation window high up on the far side of the smelly hold. Matt was speechless. He had never seen such an extraordinary contraption in his life. The inside of the submarine, when he finally made his way through to the interior, resembled ships he'd seen in very old books and films – complete with wood panelling, brass instruments and strange, rather ornate furniture.

Silas could not hide his delight and surprise at finding they had come back and he confessed to fearing that once back home on the surface the girls would have thought better of returning – let alone returning at the first opportunity, and with one of the other children he'd helped escape.

'How *are* things in Fortuna?' asked Lydia. She well remembered that when she, Polly and Lisa had left, the Polizia seemed to be making a concerted effort to surround the Southern Quarter.

'Very, very serious,' Silas replied, rubbing his beard thoughtfully. 'The Southern Quarter is more or less under siege. All the canals into and out of the area are now blocked or destroyed. I am lucky, because I can use the secret passageway leading from the Southern Quarter that ends up near my mother's home. It is now practically the only way to get in or out. To tell the truth, I'm not sure how much longer we can hold out. Anyway, you will discover that for yourselves later. I think I've found a way of getting you back into the dome without being spotted. We'll soon find out – we mustn't hang around here too long. Now then, are you all ready for the dive? I should hold on to something. This is going to be very steep.'

Just as he said it, Matt noticed the other fishing boat – far in the distance, but heading back their way. Silas dived for the controls, and following a brief shudder as he re-engaged the massive engines, the ship plunged downwards almost vertically, leaving the other boat way behind.

'That was close,' he said after a couple of minutes. 'If they had got to you before me, who knows what might have happened?'

After what seemed an age, the ship started levelling out. Polly called Matt over to the porthole she was looking through. As the ancient domed land of Fortuna gradually loomed into view, he could only stare in awe. No amount of description could have ever prepared him for the spectacle of the gigantic, translucent construction sitting on the seabed. It stretched as far as the gloomy water would allow him to see and appeared to be made of millions of crystal bricks, through which he could just make out what looked like the rooftops of a huge city. Matt gazed in wonder at the plumes of bubbles that issued from the forest of chimneys poking from the top of the dome, and the petrified landscape that surrounded its base.

'That's what happened to the rest of the land after the great flood,' explained Lydia, as if reading his mind. 'There may have been as many as a hundred towns and cities in this state. Fortuna City and its surrounding province is thought to be all that survived.'

Before returning directly to Fortuna, Silas had to make a brief detour to catch some fish in order not to create any more suspicion than he was already attracting. Everyone was impressed by how deftly Silas operated the massive jaws of the fishing craft, allowing it to scoop up shoals of plentiful silver and pink fish. When he had a viable catch in the hold, he eased the vessel down to the main fishing port at the southern perimeter of the dome and slowly approached the huge gates that led to the internal jetties.

The friends watched, spellbound, as he skilfully manoeuvred the boat towards the doors, which began to swing open at his approach. When they passed through – with only a couple of metres on either side to spare – the craft came to rest on what appeared to be an enormous rock table. At that moment, they heard a rushing noise and noticed the level of the water outside beginning to drop. In ten minutes they were high and dry beside a long jetty.

In the back of the submarine was a large stack of wicker baskets that were ready to be filled and taken on to the conveyor belt that ran along the dockside. This was how the fish would be taken to be processed and eventually distributed. Silas asked each of the young people to climb into a basket and then he and a couple of his dockside friends from the Southern Quarter piled the slimy, wriggling creatures on top of them. It was quite the most revolting sensation they had ever experienced. The baskets were then unloaded on to the quayside to await being sent to the processing plant.

Suddenly an explosion rang out from the other side of the quay. Silas, who had given one of his men a prearranged signal, smiled with satisfaction. As everyone, including the port guards, ran to see what had happened, Polly, Lisa and the others were hurriedly removed from the baskets and directed to an ordinary-looking fishing hut which had Silas's name carved above the door. Once inside and once their eyes had become accustomed to the gloom, Silas pulled a large trapdoor in the floor to one side.

Together they dropped into the hole and made their way about twenty metres along a narrow passageway to where it joined a much larger tunnel. This would lead them back to the Southern Quarter and eventually to Maricia, the old lady who had arranged their escape to the surface as babies, and who had later helped Polly and Lisa to excape again, with Lydia.

'How do you know which way to go?' Lisa asked as they hurried along after Silas, peering into all the other turnings off the tunnel.

Silas indicated almost imperceptible grooves on the wall. 'It is very important to take the correct tunnel. Take a wrong turning and it will lead you to a dead end. One way is cleverly booby-trapped. This is all to ensure that our enemies, even if they discovered this tunnel, would never be able to get out. Only those from the Southern Quarter understand the system of these markings.'

An hour or so later, they turned off into a much smaller passageway and soon found themselves at the back of a bookcase that revolved to reveal the old lady's sitting room. When the bookcase swung round, little Pietro – Silas's grandson and the boy who had first taken the girls to Maricia – ran to greet them.

'Great-grandmother will be thrilled to see you,' he squealed. 'She has been waiting for you to come back, but wasn't sure you would.'

Maricia was sitting in her armchair in front of a little fire, just as she had been when they had left her. Matt simply stared open-mouthed. Maricia, though old and exceedingly frail, had an amazing aura around her of quiet strength and determination.

'You have come back,' she chuckled quietly. 'I thought you might stay on the surface.'

'We couldn't,' said Lydia. 'We had to return to help our friends and families. We have brought another of your children back to see you. This is my twin brother Matt – or should I say, Antonio?'

The old lady grasped both of Matt's hands and held them to her pale, cool cheeks. 'You are also very brave to come here at such a crucial time. With your knowledge about the world above, you could be just what is needed to rally our people against Solon. Lydia, my dear, how did you find the world on the surface?'

'It is truly beautiful, but I found it all slightly frightening. We have these objects called photographs to show you. They are images of things that can be seen on the surface, made in a little machine. We have brought lots of them to show the people of the Southern Quarter.'

'And you have also brought a brother,' said the old lady, with a twinkle in her eye.

Lydia smiled in a shy sort of way and grasped Matt's hand. 'I don't ever want to lose him again.'

'It must be wonderful for you both,' the old lady said in a kindly voice.

'And if by any chance we could rescue our parents,' Lydia continued, 'my life would be complete.'

'I understand, my dear – but a lot has happened in the short time you have been away. The future has never been so uncertain, but I believe the planned plot to overthrow Solon and the Polizia is gaining momentum even as we speak. Isn't that right, Silas? Won't they be thrilled to have these four to help them?'

'That's right, Mother,' said Silas. 'I think having such brave youngsters amongst them will dispel any doubts they may have that now has to be the time to act. If they were prepared to come down from the surface to risk their lives for us, we certainly owe it to them to go through with the rebellion.' He turned to the others. 'I believe there will be an emergency council meeting with Theron and all the elders once they know you are here. And they should do by now, as I sent word as soon as we reached port.'

The old lady smiled, and struggled to her feet. It was only then that they realised how incredibly tall and imposing she must have been when young.

'Why don't you let my son take you up to the Southern Quarter? I think it is now time for me to reveal myself to the people there, too. For years and years I have had to be so careful. If the Polizia had had any idea where I was, they would have raided the Southern Quarter sooner. We could not take the risk. But there is no point concealing my identity any longer.'

Chapter 6

LITTLE PIETRO TROTTED TO the revolving bookcase and led the four visitors into the narrow and
almost pitch-black tunnel that Polly, Lisa and Lydia
had used on that fateful day when he had first con-
tacted them. This led, after a short distance, into the
main network of well-lit passageways that crisscrossed
underneath most of the Southern Quarter. When they
emerged at ground level, poor Matt couldn't believe his
eyes. He had been told at great length of the beauty of
Fortuna, with its lofty fountains, spiralling waterways,
hanging gardens and magnificent ornate buildings, but
all he was able to see now were the dismal, water-soaked
buildings of the Southern Quarter. They had to keep
close to the edges of the buildings to reduce the risk of
being seen by enemy eyes, but Matt could only stare in
dismay at such a totally awful place – buildings covered

in thick, green slime; mist swirling way, way above; a slow, soaking drizzle and a host of blacked out windows that seemed to look at, and follow, the new intruders like ghostly eyes. There was no life to be seen apart from a few damp rats, skulking in the shadows.

'Is all the Southern Quarter like this?' whispered Matt, almost too horrified to speak.

'Just wait until we get inside,' replied Polly. 'It's not what it seems.'

Pietro led them through dim, dank passages and up rickety staircases for what seemed ages, but as they climbed higher, the passageways became lighter and more colourful. People, dressed in tattered but stylish and brightly-coloured robes, on recognising Lydia, Polly and Lisa, greeted them warmly and patted them on the back.

Eventually they came to the great hall where Theron and the full council of the Southern Quarter were waiting. Matt was amazed. If the outside of the building had looked sad and neglected, the inside, although in need of restoration, showed how magnificent this place had once been. Lofty pillars held up an impressive vaulted ceiling covered in plaster cherubs and painted scenes from Greek mythology. Round the walls and set into alcoves were statues of what he assumed must be famous dignitaries from the distant past.

Word had obviously got through that the young

people were back from the surface, for their reception was nothing short of rapturous. Hundreds of Fortunans of all ages, pressed forward to catch a glimpse. The applause continued until the tall, majestic figure of Theron stepped forward and raised his hand.

'May I, on behalf of all the good people of the Southern Quarter, welcome you back to help us in our hour of need. You are very, very brave. Things have certainly got worse since you left. We are now completely surrounded by Solon's Polizia and we expect a full-blown attack at any time. We have not been idle, however. Since you have been away, we have not only made preparations to defend ourselves but also to launch a fully structured attack to finally put a halt to this hateful regime. With luck, Solon will be too busy thinking about closing down the Southern Quarter to even consider a huge rebellion within his own city.'

Theron paused, looking grave. 'We have a detailed plan of action, but we need to get as many people as possible throughout Fortuna City to help the cause too. We realise we may have very little time, but in a way that is good. The longer we leave it, the more chance Solon has of hearing of our plans. If we can get everyone fully prepared for the conflict, we might be able to defeat the Polizia. The advantage we have is that everyone here is prepared to die for their cause – this makes us very powerful. You see, we have no choice. If we don't take a stand, it will soon be the end of us. We will be vanquished.'

Lydia, who appeared unphased by the occasion, spoke next in a loud, clear voice, addressing the assembly. 'May I introduce my twin brother, Matt. He was called Antonio when he first left our world as a baby. I had not seen him since then. He has lived up on the surface ever since and has come down to help us.'

Loud applause filled the hall, and their leader raised his hands to silence them.

'Does anyone on the surface know what we are facing?' Theron asked the group.

Lisa, who felt far less nervous than she would have imagined, replied. 'We have only told certain people about the existence of Fortuna, but there are very good reasons for this which we can tell you about later. All we can say for sure is that if – sorry, *when* – you beat Solon, there will be a welcome on the surface for anyone who wants to go there.' She swallowed deeply, hoping she had just told the truth. She could only assume that this would be the case. 'We have brought you pictures of the world above should anyone still not believe it really exists.'

She and Polly had also brought their cameras with a few selected videos on them. The audience crowded round them and looked on in wonder. Not only had they never heard of photographs or videos but they had never seen cameras either.

Theron clapped his hands and laughed. 'My sources tell me you had rather an unconventional arrival today. You must be exhausted. Perhaps you would like to rest and come back to us later. We have a machine which can project your images to a great size. I have no doubt it will be the most exciting event we have ever witnessed and should be all we need to spur us on for the great conflict to come.'

The four new arrivals were acutely aware of their filthy state and fishy smell. Polly and Lisa looked round, hoping that the gorgeous boy Balia would be there to escort them to their quarters as he had done the first time, but he was nowhere to be seen.

Theron seemed to read their minds. 'I am sorry to have to tell you that we think that Balia, who you met on your last visit, was captured on the outer perimeter of the Southern Quarter soon after you left. He was on a mission to discover the strength of the enemy army surrounding us. We have no idea where he is or indeed whether he is still alive. I am terribly sorry.'

Hearing this news suddenly brought the immediacy of this dangerous situation to the visitors, and they all felt a shiver go through their bodies.

'How many people have you lost so far?' asked Lydia.

Theron looked serious. 'We don't know if the people that are missing have been killed or sent to Devilla. It is difficult to say which is worse.'

One of Theron's right-hand men spoke up. 'We cannot delay and must beat them to action. Surprise is our greatest weapon. I think we must set a day now and let everyone know so that they can be ready.'

Theron looked doubtful. 'It is a huge risk. If it gets through to any of Solon's spies we are finished.'

'We must make sure that the plan is only passed on to people who can be really trusted. Once it is out there, I believe we only have a matter of days, if that,' added another council member.

Theron suddenly took control. 'I think the rebellion should be set for ten days from now. Does anyone disagree?'

'How will we let everyone know, with all the canals cut off?' came a voice from the crowd.

Another voice came from the back of the hall. 'There is the tunnel that leads from the Southern Quarter to the fishing port. From there we can move throughout Fortuna.'

Every head turned towards the voice to see Silas the fisherman, with, to everyone's surprise, an ancient lady on his arm – an ancient lady whom only the four youngsters recognised.

'This, ladies and gentlemen, is my mother Maricia – the brave woman who is responsible for our young friends coming down to help us today.'

A complete silence fell on hall as they all stared

at the frail old lady who had been no more than a rumour for years. Her exploits had been legendary and indeed, few believed her to be still alive. And then from nowhere it began. It started with a slow, slightly nervous handclap and then built to a most tumultuous cheer that dwarfed anything that had ever been heard in the room before.

The old lady, helped by her son, hobbled slowly and painfully through the cheering throng to the raised platform, where she was lifted by a sea of helping hands. She raised her arm and a sudden hush fell over the whole hall. She then spoke, in her thin, breathy voice. 'People of the Southern Quarter, I thank you. I feel honoured to be amongst you in your hour of need. As you know, I have kept my identity secret for many years because of the work I have been doing – first with my dear husband and then with my brave son, Silas. Now I believe it is time for us to rally together to overthrow the wicked Solon, or perish in the process. Fortuna was once a beautiful land, full of light and culture. Now it is a cruel, sinister place where only those who abide by the rules and do as Solon demands can flourish. Those that don't, as you know, either live here – if they are lucky – or are subjected to a life of abject misery in Devilla. It is our task to make Fortuna beautiful again. We have ten days to prepare.'

* * *

Lydia and her three friends were escorted to Theron's very own quarters where a special suite had been prepared for them. In the centre of the room was a low table with a wide selection of appetising-looking food and drink – including rat-burgers, a speciality of the Southern Quarter that Polly and Lisa remembered from their last visit. The young people were so hungry, however, that they didn't even question the origin of what had been put out for them. When they had bathed in the wonderful Roman-style baths, they put on the clothes that had been hung out for them. Though not what they would have chosen to wear at home, they all agreed that the bright colours and abstract shapes reminded them of what had been worn in the hippy era that their grandparents back on the surface had described.

That evening, the girls showed the photographs of the world they had left behind – from cities to mountain ranges, from cars to aeroplanes to everything they had thought would be of interest to an audience who had never seen the earth above. The contraption to project pictures that Theron had told them about was very ingenious. It consisted of a series of magnifying lenses and mirrors, linked to an intense gas light that threw the images on to the far wall.

The gasps of excitement and wonder from the audience were unmistakable, as one by one the photos explained a way of life that had until relatively recently been just a vague rumour. Towards the end, they had chosen to include some pictures that were not quite so flattering – pictures of huge guns, explosions, armies and, worst of all, emaciated, starving children.

Polly explained, 'The earlier pictures you have just seen show a wonderful world full of lots of lovely things and brilliant places. This all exists, of course, but it is only one side of life on the surface of the earth. We also have many cruel and awful people, just like your Solon, who try to make the others do as they want. The result of this is that many, many poor people suffer and often starve.'

Lisa took over. 'And we are told that the surface is suffering from the results of too many of the vehicles you saw in the pictures, and too many factories producing gases that are in danger of damaging the protective layer that keeps the sun from burning us up. In a way we are facing what you are facing, but not quite as urgently.'

'We are only telling you all this in case you think that life on the surface is perfect,' Polly interjected. 'For every person who has a good life, with enough to eat and a nice home to live in, there are many who go hungry and live in the most appalling squalor.'

When it was clear that Polly had finished, Theron stepped up on to the platform next to the young visitors.

'I think you have been very fair and very honest. Despite the drawbacks you describe, it is nice to know that there is somewhere we could go if things became impossible here. But I, for one, love Fortuna, even though I can't remember a time when we were free from crushing cruelty. We will fight together to return it to how it used to be before Solon's dynasty came to power – a time when everyone worked for the good of the community, a time before hundreds of our brothers and sisters were forced into slavery.'

His final words were drowned by the rapturous clapping and cheering of the crowd.

Chapter 7

THE FOLLOWING DAY, POLLY, Lisa, Matt and Lydia were invited to meet again with the leaders of the Southern Quarter to hear what was planned. Theron and his advisors had been sending out small groups whose job it was to infiltrate the Fortunans, telling them to be prepared for the great rebellion. He had left this late in order that there would be less chance of Solon hearing about it. But this mission had been increasingly difficult to perform as leaving or coming back to the Southern Quarter was almost impossible, owing to the ring of Polizia who had a stranglehold on all the canals. Silas's tunnel would make it much easier. Theron had thought it better to target the young people of Fortuna and so had asked for more volunteers from amongst the young of the Southern Quarter. When they heard, Polly and Lisa instantly asked to join them, telling Theron that they could take their cameras and photographs as proof of a more advanced culture above the ocean and distribute printed photos amongst the other volunteers.

The rebel forces, Theron explained, were to attack all the key areas of Fortunan society simultaneously, concentrating on the main centres of administration and, most important of all, the huge underground factories that provided the city's power and light. For that he had organised small, highly trained squads, but they hoped they would be helped by Fortunans who would be sympathetic to their struggle. The ultimate aim, Theron continued, was to capture Solon, as with him deposed his whole evil regime would tumble.

First of all, however, Theron was determined to liberate the poor people of Devilla, as soon as possible. To facilitate this he realised that he must infiltrate their numbers so that they could at least be ready for what was about to happen and help when the time came. If they had proof of a world above it would be made easier. Before the four friends came back to Fortuna, he had asked for volunteers to go to Devilla, but as yet nobody had come forward. Everyone in the Southern Quarter knew just how terrible things were there and the idea of possibly being caught and forced to spend the rest of their life in that hell was too daunting.

When Matt and Lydia heard of Theron's plea for

volunteers, they begged to be allowed to go. At first he dismissed their request, saying that he could never live with himself if anything happened to them – Theron had always treated Lydia as if she were his own daughter. Gradually, however, they persuaded him that they were probably the best qualified to rally the inmates of Devilla, having first-hand knowledge not only of the planned rebellion, but of the world above.

Although many of those in the Southern Quarter knew roughly where Devilla was located, few had ever dared to go near the place – for obvious reasons. Despite Theron's misgivings, Polly and Lisa who had accidentally stumbled upon the dreadful prison on their first visit, suggested they could take Lydia and Matt there. They would also be able to take photographs to show the terrible state of the prisoners which would surely be useful when it came to convincing Fortunans to join the rebels.

After much discussion, a plan was agreed. Matt and Lydia were to be disguised as slaves and would infiltrate the column of people returning to Devilla from their daily labours. Some sort of diversion would have to be thought up to distract the guards. Theron wondered if there would be a head count as they returned, but reasoned that the idea that anyone could possibly want to break *into* Devilla had probably never occurred to them. Even if they did, the guards would most likely put any small discrepancy in numbers down to human error. Theron then assured the two brave volunteers that even if things did go wrong for them in Devilla, his newly-formed army would dedicate themselves to storming Devilla and rescuing all who were imprisoned there.

When the friends awoke the following day after a restless night's sleep, they could hear strange whoomfing noises and thought that perhaps the Polizia's attack on the Southern Quarter had already begun. It was only when they were brought breakfast that they found out it was simply weapon practice. Over the last few years, the brilliant engineers of the Southern Quarter had not only invented but had also been manufacturing a stockpile of simple but effective weapons. Now practically everyone was being taught to use them.

Later, the four of them walked through towards the main hall and were amazed to see men, women and children lying on the ground at one end, firing at targets. The weapons, though extremely powerful, were designed not to kill but to stun, and were much quieter than any they'd heard before. This was because, unlike conventional guns, which were powered by an explosive charge, these were powered by air pressure. The air in the barrel was compressed by a simple lever mechanism and, on release, a thin column of air would shoot out at such velocity that anything in its path would be floored.

Theron smiled. 'We've all had enough of killing. This way we can render our enemies unconscious long enough to restrain them.'

They were all allowed to try their hand and were surprised at how accurate the weapons were.

'I've never even seen a real gun close-up before, let alone one like this,' said Lisa.

'Me neither,' said Polly. 'It's all right doing this, I suppose, because these weapons don't kill, but I'm still not sure I could actually use one against anyone. I've never purposely hurt anything in my life.'

Matt laughed sarcastically. 'Tell you what, Poll, if it was a choice between me or some crazy maniac in a uniform pointing a real gun at me, I'd be damned sure *I'd* use it.'

'I suppose you're right,' said Polly. 'It just seems terrible to come to this.'

Matt suddenly looked angry. 'Listen, Poll, if you've any doubt left, just think of your real parents. You'll be lucky if they're still alive.'

Chapter 8

TWO DAYS LATER, as darkness fell, Matt, Lydia, Polly and Lisa said their goodbyes and made their way carefully through Silas's tunnel to the fishing port. They were all dressed in the streamlined swimsuits that the women in the Southern Quarter had become so skilled in making. They took photos and a camera with them in their waterproof backpacks, along with filthy rags that had been prepared for Matt and Lydia.

As they made their way in the darkness, using the canal from the fishing port, they were surprised not to come across a single Polizia patrol. Then they worked out that most of them would be surrounding the Southern Quarter. Lisa was the first to spot the sinister lights of the Devilla buildings, with their high watchtowers at either end. When they were a hundred or so metres away, they left the water and Matt and Lydia slipped into the filthy rags and hid photos underneath them.

The four adventurers then crept behind the first hut, careful to avoid the watchful eye of the guard on the nearest watchtower. They then sat down and waited for the end of the darkness, knowing that it had always been the policy of the overlords of Fortuna to keep the prisoners underground during the period of light so that they would not be seen by citizens. After a while, they heard what they had been waiting for. It was like the distant rumble of marching – not ordered, military marching, but more muffled and ponderous. They peered round the far side of the hut and could just make out a long column of dishevelled, broken people of all ages shuffling silently towards them along the dusty track, worn deep and smooth by years of dragging footsteps. The only other sounds were the occasional barking of orders and sharp cracking of whips from the guards who were walking beside them. Matt and Lydia mouthed their goodbyes to Polly and Lisa who, having taken as many photographs as they could of the sad column, quickly made their way back to the canals.

As soon as the two girls had left, it was time for the next part of the plan. Matt took out the small, walnut-sized grenade, given to him by the scientists of the Southern Quarter with the instruction to make sure he threw it as far away as possible. Shaking, Matt pulled the tiny pin which started the timer and flung the contraption as far as he could into an unoccupied part of the encampment.

The size of the ensuing explosion took even him by surprise and soon the guards were running towards the plume of smoke that hung in the air above the prison. It was now or never. Matt and Lydia threw themselves past the watchtower and slipped in amongst the column of miserable workers. They had been nervous in case the prisoners made a commotion, but the people were so exhausted they hardly noticed they had been joined. Any idea of escaping had been drummed out of them and all they could do was stand and stare at the running guards.

Chapter 9

POLLY AND LISA COULDN'T afford to hang around to watch their friends join the prisoners. Instead they slipped back to find a canal that looked as if it might be flowing south. For all they knew they might never see Matt and Lydia again and were hardly able to speak for the worry they felt. After a while the lights had come up fully and they were able to see the city in the distance.

Their plan had been to make their way gradually back towards the Southern Quarter, circulating the news of what was about to happen, the information on the world above and the horror of Devilla to any young Fortunans that they came across on the way. Any doubts as to the truth of their claims would be dispelled by the photographs they carried in their cameras. They felt sure that the ones they had just taken of the tragic column of prisoners would be enough to persuade anyone of the evils of the current regime.

There were, as they had thought, many small bands of youths about, who seemed well aware that *something* was going on, but appeared to have no idea as to what it could be. Indeed, Polly and Lisa's audiences became so excited when they heard about the prospect of another world above the surface that they began to ask a whole host of questions. This was an encouraging response, for the youth of Fortuna had always been forbidden from asking questions about anything.

Part of Polly and Lisa's job was to make it perfectly clear that the rebellion could not fail to succeed, even if they did have their own personal doubts as to whether the legendary Solon could be vanquished. The two girls had also been told by Theron to finish each encounter with a severe warning, to the effect that anyone who reported what they had been told to the authorities would be dealt with severely by the new regime. The young people they told were to use their discretion where their parents were concerned.

Just south of the city, Polly and Lisa came across a much larger group of young people by one of the lakes. It turned out they too had heard all sorts of rumours of something momentous that was about to happen, but as yet knew little. They all became silent and eyed the two young strangers extremely suspiciously as they approached.

'Hello,' Lisa began, in a quiet but confident voice. 'Me and my friend have come from the Southern Quarter and have something important to tell you.'

That in itself was a bombshell. Their audience looked apprehensive at first and then downright scared. They had always been told that anyone from the Southern Quarter looked and acted like a barbarian. Polly and Lisa, however, did not seem remotely threatening – although they had strange accents, they looked so like them with their blond hair, green eyes and streamlined costumes.

'We have come to tell you that there are to be some enormous changes. Some you may like, some you may not,' Lisa went on.

'What sort of changes?' asked a tall boy of about seventeen, with a sneer. 'Who are you to talk like this?'

Lisa smiled but ignored the question. 'Have you ever wondered how you manage to live in such luxury, without anyone ever seeming to have to work?'

The group looked at each other and, although they seemed to be pretending not to understand the question, looked slightly embarrassed. They'd been brainwashed into never questioning the regime.

'Are you aware,' she continued, 'that there are hundreds of people kept in a huge underground prison, and that they only come out at dark-time to do all the jobs that keep you and your parents in the luxurious style you are used to?'

A couple of the youths looked more embarrassed than the others and made as if to walk away, but their friends blocked their passage, forcing them to stay.

'How do you know this?' asked the same boy, indignantly. 'It sounds ridiculous to me, but even if it were true, it probably serves them right.'

'You have been deceived by the ruling class,' said Polly. 'Now we are telling you the awful truth and are warning you that you had better believe it. Everyone in the Southern Quarter has known about Devilla, the prison, for years and years. Many have friends and relatives there, as do the rest of the Fortunans.'

The group began arguing urgently amongst themselves until Lisa called them to order. 'Look, Solon is a monster. We know because we've met him. He will do anything and get rid of anyone to stay in power. We believe that all who support him are as guilty as he is.'

The whole group looked horrified to hear Solon spoken of in such a way. Any person in the past who even vaguely criticised his regime would disappear mysteriously.

The sneering boy came back. 'You're not one of those girls who claim they come from some place above the water, are you? We have heard strange rumours.'

'So you *have* heard of us,' said Lisa with a faint

smile. 'Yes, we are. We were taken up there as babies. We believe our parents were sent to Devilla purely for having us, so they could well be dead by now – worked to death. Anyway, it is true – there *is* a whole world up there. We are sure Solon is aware of this, but doesn't want the people of Fortuna to know in case they might all want to leave. If they did, his reign would tumble immediately.'

'What is it like up there?' asked a young girl from the back.

Polly and Lisa spent the next half hour explaining once again a world that bore little resemblance to the one their audience was familiar with. They talked them into a complete silence and that was before showing them the photographs and videos on their cameras. Lisa then dropped their final bombshell.

'In a few days' time, when the lights come on, there is to be a rebellion larger by far than anything that has ever been known in the whole history of Fortuna. It will be led by the brave people of the Southern Quarter and we advise you strongly to join us. It cannot be done any other way. What we are doing is right . . . that we know. When, or rather if, you tell your parents, you must warn them that if they go to the authorities they will be dealt with extremely harshly by the new regime.'

'Are you threatening us?' demanded the tall boy, now angry and becoming threatening himself.

Lisa rose to her full height and stared at him menacingly. 'Take it how you like, you idiot. The days of half the population slaving for people like you will soon be over, whether you like it or not. All those poor slaves I mentioned will be released and taken to the Southern Quarter where they will be cared for until they have recovered from their terrible ordeal. An emergency government will be put in place of Solon, who will be made to pay for his crimes. You have been warned. Now tell all your friends, but be aware of Solon's spies.'

The young people were left stunned and scared, but strangely excited. There was something about Polly and Lisa's manner that made them realise that this rebellion might really happen and that the most important thing was to be on the winning side. Many of them even realised that ending such cruelty might be the right thing to do.

Polly and Lisa left the young people talking urgently amongst themselves and made their way towards the fishing village and to Silas's tunnel. The two girls were only a few minutes away when they heard someone calling out behind them. Whirling around, they realised that, instead of being alone, they were now the centre of unwanted attention. They had been spotted by one of the few Polizia patrols around.

The two girls cast about frantically for an escape route but this time there was nowhere to go. Half a dozen heavily armed men were surrounding them.

'What are you two doing?' barked a tall, ugly man who they presumed to be in charge. 'You know the rules. You are not allowed this far from the city perimeter. Wait a minute,' he snarled, 'haven't I seen you two before? Aren't you the girls we've had orders to arrest on sight?'

The captain, realising the praise and promotion he would no doubt receive for bringing them in, didn't even wait for a reply but ordered his men to seize them. This time Polly and Lisa were handled far less graciously than when they'd first arrived in Fortuna. They were roughly tied together and thrown unceremoniously into the back of the patrol boat, where they were held by the arms on either side by Polizia. Neither had to think very hard where they would be taken and whom they would no doubt be forced to meet.

'Don't even ask me if I'm scared this time,' whispered Lisa. 'I reckon Solon'll go beserk.'

'Do you think he'll send us to Devilla?' asked Polly with a trembling voice.

Lisa stared straight into her best friend's frightened eyes, but was lost for words.

Half an hour later, they were pushed into Solon's vast state room. The old man was pacing up and down in a fury, his carved walking stick rapping the ground rhythmically. The room was just as they remembered it, with its high ornate ceilings and huge windows looking out over the city. Solon looked every bit the governor in his long black tunic, totally plain apart from a large chain with a silver fish hanging from it. This fish was the symbol that they knew so well – the symbol that had started the whole discovery of who they really were.

Solon's wizened old face was twisted into a mask of pure hatred as he pulled himself up to his full height. 'So here you are!' he snarled, banging his stick on the floor. 'I suppose there is little point asking where you have been?'

When they'd talked about him back on the surface, Polly and Lisa had both agreed that Solon would suppose they had been hiding in the Southern Quarter during their absence from his city. The question seemed to confirm their guess.

'We would have got you eventually,' he continued maliciously, 'when we finally overthrow the Southern Quarter and put an end to that old crone who delivered you to the surface. The Southern Quarter will soon no longer exist and its population of thieves and murderers will either be terminated or sent to Devilla. As for you two, you are of no further use to me now, so you will be disposed of in the most appropriate fashion.'

The two friends held on to each other in pure terror as he hobbled right up to them. 'My men found these in your little bags.' He thrust their cameras at them. 'What do they do?'

Polly and Lisa glanced at each other and then looked to the floor and shrugged as if they had no idea.

The old man whacked his stick on the ground so hard sparks flew from the metal tip. 'You will tell me now!' he screamed. 'You might as well, as you cannot make things worse for yourselves.'

Lisa was shaking so much she could hardly operate the little camera. She took a picture of Polly and showed it to Solon, whose eyes opened wide in wonder. He then tore it from her hand and almost intuitively pressed the scroll-back button. When he saw the image of the line of prisoners with Devilla's prison buildings in the background, he flung it to the ground as if it was inhabited by some evil spirit.

'So you have been to Devilla. You really are far more dangerous than even I supposed. You must have thought I was very naive,' he spat. 'Of course I always knew about your world above. It is, and always has been, all that really threatens my power down here in Fortuna. If the people up there were to find out about us they would try to change things. I'm sure you know what I mean. You two were the only link to that world and we knew that it had only been made possible by that old witch, Maricia. I have been trying for years to find her. When you two arrived, we were sure you would lead us to her. Why else would I have kept you alive? That's why we let you out on such a loose rein with my most important man, Petruvio, as your guardian. Now I suppose everyone in the Southern Quarter knows of the world above. If they could somehow make contact with the surface dwellers, they could tell all. Our wonderful life would be over.'

Lisa suddenly found her voice in the most extraordinary manner. 'Soon everyone in the whole of Fortuna will also know that it is only you and your people who have been keeping the other world from them.'

'Be silent, you deluded young idiot!' the old man screamed at the top of his still-powerful voice and raised his stick as if to strike her. 'I cannot imagine the trouble you've caused. For some reason your coming seems to have boosted the rebels' confidence, and our idyllic society here is threatened.'

Polly, who up to that point had been riveted to the ground with pure fear, suddenly saw red herself and found a loud angry voice she never knew she had. 'Oh yes, very idyllic,' she mocked, 'with half of your people being kept as slaves so that the rest can live a life of luxury.'

Solon shook his old head. 'You stupid, stupid child. You could have had that luxury for yourself. People who break the law and threaten my authority are simply animals and will always be treated as such. Now I realise that you are both far too dangerous to even be kept alive. You will be imprisoned in our dungeons below – but only until we have found out everything we need to know. Believe me, if you know anything at all, you would be well advised to tell my men straight away.'

'We will tell you nothing,' cried Lisa belligerently. 'Besides, what would be the point if you're going to kill us anyway?' As she said this the full implications of the situation hit her and she began to tremble uncontrollably, despite her anger.

Solon laughed a horrible, whiny laugh. 'Oh I don't think I need worry too much about that. We have ways of getting the strongest, bravest individuals to tell all, even about their own families. You two will be easy, believe me. In fact, I am confident you will be sorry you ever resisted. Now get out of my sight.'

He turned his back as two huge guards stepped forward to take the petrified girls to the dungeons below. This time they were dragged along the corridor to an ominous black studded door, beyond which was a special water-lift that plummeted vertically until it came to a sudden jolting halt way below Solon's quarters.

Polly and Lisa were pushed out of the lift into the semi-darkness of the most horribly depressing dungeon cell they could have imagined. Its walls, which appeared to have been hewn from the solid rock, were green with slime and glistened with the rivulets of water that dribbled from the ceiling. There were no creature comforts whatsoever, not even a bench to sit on.

'Oh God,' whispered Lisa, on the verge of tears, as the guards slammed the cell door shut and walked away. 'What on earth have we done?'

Polly was sobbing. 'Do you really think he's going to kill us?'

'We've got to get out of here,' muttered Lisa, ignoring the question. Even as she said it, she looked doubtfully round at the walls. 'The trouble is, the only way out seems to be the way in.'

She walked over to the door and noticed that more heavy bars had swung across the gap which led to the lift. Then, just to make things even worse, the little light which had illuminated their dingy cell went out, leaving them in total darkness. Polly and Lisa fell to the ground and clung to each other in pure terror.

Chapter 10

WHILE WAITING IN THE queue of prisoners for the guards to return, Matt and Lydia had a brief opportunity to look around them as the light had almost fully returned. From the outside, the entrance to Devilla looked quite inconspicuous and not particularly menacing – just a scattering of buildings within a quadrangle with large gates which opened as the column approached. There were four watchtowers, one at each corner, each with armed guards. In the distance were larger buildings that looked like factories, with tall chimneys rising towards the ceiling of the dome.

When the puzzled guards returned from trying to find the source of the explosion, Matt and Lydia were made to march slowly, surrounded by the exhausted, foul-smelling inhabitants. They filed past dragging their feet and creating a cloud of choking dust which hovered ominously above their heads. After a while Lydia and Matt noticed a fairly small building ahead of them into which the column was slowly disappearing. It was obvious that this building would soon have been full if it didn't have some sort of underground tunnel or space into which the people could be absorbed.

Eventually it was their turn to enter and as soon as they were inside they found it was as they had guessed. They began to descend a wide, spiral staircase. At the bottom, in the close, dank, semi-darkness, they came across what looked like a railway platform at which a series of open carriages were waiting. As each carriage was crammed full of prisoners, the train moved along just far enough to allow the next one to be filled. Eventually, when the last carriage was loaded, the train chugged out of the underground station, leaving behind a trail of choking, acrid smoke.

As they looked round in the carriage, Lydia noticed that although nobody else seemed to have registered the arrival of two new people, one particular woman had been staring at her and her brother for some time. Lydia met her gaze full-on as if challenging her to speak. When she didn't, Lydia decided to take her courage in both hands.

'Who are you?' she whispered, just loud enough to be heard over the rattle of the train wheels.

The woman looked petrified. 'Don't speak here, it's

forbidden. People have been terminated for less. I will find you later,' she whispered urgently, disappearing into the crush of people.

The train eventually began to slow down and Matt and Lydia found themselves moving into a large subterranean hall, full of people hunched at rows of tables as far as the eye could see. There was no noise apart from the squealing of the wheels as the train drew to a halt each time it returned with more workers. As the two of them alighted from the train, they searched for spaces at the tables. It was then that Matt and Lydia noticed another smell apart from that of sweaty, unwashed bodies. Looking to the far end of the hall they could just make out a huge iron cauldron, shrouded in steam. Several guards appeared to be distributing large lumps of what looked like black bread and bowls containing what turned out to be a thick, unappetising broth. One by one, the crowd dragged themselves to the end of the hall and took the only sustenance they would have had all day.

They ate mostly in silence and, when they had finished, made their way towards a huge set of doors halfway along the bare stone walls. Lydia noticed the strange woman had appeared, as she had promised, right beside them. Neither she nor her brother could stomach the broth and gave theirs to a couple next to them, eating only the rough gritty bread. Eventually a siren sounded and the woman beckoned them to join the queue that was filtering out through the doors and into a long gloomy corridor which stretched into the darkness.

To either side of this corridor were doors with numbers above them. When they were about halfway along, the woman grabbed Lydia roughly by the arm and pulled her through one of them. She noticed the number thirty-seven above the door. Matt only just managed to avoid being dragged along by the rest of the crowd and followed his sister through the open door. Inside were about twenty other people, lying on straw mattresses. None of them seemed to notice the new arrivals, being too tired to pay much attention to anything. When the last mattress was taken, one of the prisoners walked to the door, almost like a robot, and pushed it closed.

The woman spoke first in a quiet but determined voice. 'Who are you?'

'Don't worry,' said Lydia quietly, 'we are not here to spy on you or harm you. We are from the outside.'

'The outside? What do you mean, the outside?' she asked suspiciously. 'How did you come to be here?'

Lydia noticed that several of the other inmates had heard her speaking and were slowly rousing themselves.

'It's a long story,' said Lydia, 'but we joined the column coming in. We are searching for our parents.'

'Are you completely mad?' said the woman, almost sneering. 'Nobody comes here voluntarily. Your parents are probably dead. Either way, you will never escape now you're here.'

Matt shuddered at the prospect. 'There is to be a massive rebellion above,' he said quietly. 'We are here to tell you to be ready.'

By this time everyone in the room had gathered round.

An old man spoke from the back. 'Rebellion, you say? What can we do? We are all too weak to fight. Anyway, we have no weapons.'

'You simply have to be ready,' said Lydia gently. 'Help will come to you.'

'But why now? What is so different?' asked the woman who had first spoken. She was still deeply suspicious.

Matt explained that he was from the surface, and showed the astounded inmates a few of the photographs of the world above that he had smuggled in under his ragged shirt. As they were passed round in the dim light, most of the exhausted inmates simply stared at them incomprehensibly, failing to take the images in.

'When is this rebellion going to happen?' asked a thin young man, who seemed to understand what they were saying. 'What can we do?'

Lydia raised her hand. 'Stay calm and act as if nothing

has happened. Tell everybody to try as hard as possible to conserve their energy and to circulate this news to the rest of the prisoners.'

'How can we? We're not allowed to talk outside here,' muttered an older lady, who was so tired she could hardly make her voice heard.

'You'll just have to take a chance. Try and speak when the guards are nowhere near you. Remember, if they get wind of it, the only chance you will ever have to be free will be gone.'

'We must tell Helena and Christos,' the young man said quietly.

'Who are they?' asked Lydia.

'They do their best to keep our spirits up. They are always trying to think of ways to escape.'

'Can we meet them?' asked Matt.

'It is difficult to meet anyone here, especially them. They are being watched all the time. It is a miracle that they haven't been terminated already.'

The next hour was spent trying to explain to people who had spent most of their lives underground what life was like on the surface. The woman who had led them into the room spoke in a much kinder and gentler voice when they had finished.

'To have left there to come to save us makes you quite the bravest young people I have ever come across, and I salute you and most humbly apologise. I am so sorry I spoke like I did. Living here makes you very hard and suspicious of everyone. If I can help you find out about your parents I will. I have been in Devilla nearly all of my life. My parents were terminated simply for having me. I have always said I would be prepared to die in the pursuit of freedom if there was the slightest chance of success. The moment I saw you I realised that you had not been here long. It's in your eyes – they are bright and alert. Look at these poor people around you.'

Matt and Lydia surveyed the deep-set, exhausted eyes staring at them, none with the slightest spark of light.

At that point there was a rap on the door, and the prisoners heard the guard outside ordering them to be silent.

Chapter 11

POLLY AND LISA, DEEP in their subterranean prison, were on the verge of total despair. They had returned to Fortuna against their instincts to find their real parents, and now it looked as if they would not only never live to see them, but that they wouldn't see their adoptive parents again either. Neither had been more frightened in their lives. For a start, they had no idea when and where they would be taken to be interrogated, let alone what form it would take. And then . . . What might happen next didn't bear thinking about.

'We should never have come back,' said Lisa in a tiny voice, which still managed to echo round their cell. 'You were right, Poll. I am so, so sorry.'

'It might have been all right had we kept our wits about us. How did we not see that Polizia patrol?'

'It makes no difference now. How long do you think

they'll keep us here before . . . ?' She could not even bear to finish the sentence.

Polly began to sob quietly again while Lisa held her best friend close and stroked her hair.

They had been clinging together, shivering in the clammy darkness for several long hours, when they finally heard the sound they were dreading – the sound of the lift approaching. They stared at each other in the dark as the realisation of what was about to occur dawned on them. As the light filled their cell, they hugged each other tearfully as if to say goodbye. Holding their breath, they waited to see who or what would come through the lift gates. When the doors swung back, their mouths fell open. They were completely and utterly staggered to see the handsome face of Petruvio, their old guardian. Their minds raced. Had he been sent to torture or kill them? The last time they had escaped from him he must have been in severe trouble with Solon. Perhaps he had volunteered for the job of interrogating them to make it up to him. He would no doubt take great pleasure in seeing them suffer.

The two girls cowered in the corner as he approached, but both sensed something was different in his expression. Instead of the slightly superior look they had been used to, Petruvio stared at the two girls and looked as if he too were about to break down.

'I'm so, so relieved you're still here and not hurt,' he

exclaimed. 'I heard you had been caught and got here as quickly as I could. Solon, my uncle, has no idea I even know where the dungeons are. Look, we haven't long. Are you ready?'

'R-ready for what?' stammered Lisa, trying her best to hold back the tears. The last time they had seen Petruvio, he had been furious with them.

'I must get you out of here. They will be coming for you soon to interrogate you and then . . . then . . . I simply cannot allow it. They are horribly cruel.'

Polly and Lisa were completely confused. They had always known that Petruvio was Solon's faithful nephew and therefore a sworn enemy. How could they now be expected to trust him?

'Look, there's no time to explain. You must trust me or you will be terminated – that much I'm sure of. Come with me now and ask questions later. Please, please, I beg of you!'

The girls stared at each other, but didn't need asking twice. Anything had to be better than waiting in the cold and dark for an unknown fate. They followed Petruvio to the lift and, once inside, it began to ascend. When the lift was only halfway up, Petruvio pulled a lever, causing it to come to a halt.

'I hope you two are able to keep up,' he said with the hint of a smile. He prised the door open a few centimetres and waited for the water to flood in.

When it was full to the top and they were all totally submerged, he opened the door completely, swam out and beckoned the girls to follow him up a vertical column of murky water until he came to a small hatch which he slid open. Both girls felt terribly claustrophobic as they half crawled, half swam along the narrow, water-filled tunnel behind Petruvio. After what seemed an age, the tunnel opened, surprisingly, into the bottom of a small pool that turned out to be in one of the city's main squares.

They floated to the surface and sat on the side for a few moments to get their breath back. Petruvio then spoke urgently.

'I am so relieved I got to you in time. We must make for the Southern Quarter. I don't know how the people there will treat me, though. They must know that Solon is my uncle.'

'Why are you doing this?' asked Polly. 'We thought you hated us.'

Petruvio looked very serious. 'It was difficult for me when I was put in charge of you. I'd suspected for some time that Solon had been, and still was, a cruel tyrant, but I had been brainwashed like so many of the people of Fortuna. I was frightened to talk to you because of what you might say. I was being trained, you see, to be his second-in-command. I was forced to act when my spy in the Southern Quarter told me of the planned rebellion. It was time to make a decision and I did. Instead of going to my uncle, I realised I wanted to help the rebels. It is only a matter of time before Solon gets to hear of this and orders my arrest and execution. So, in a way, girls, I am in the same boat as you now, you see.' The handsome young man smiled. 'Talking of boats, we must find one and head south right away.'

Lisa looked very serious. Could they really trust Petruvio? She cast a look over to Polly who, as always, knew exactly what her best friend was thinking. She nodded slowly.

'We've heard that all the canals going into the Southern Quarter are either blocked or destroyed,' Lisa said. 'Nobody can get in or out by normal routes. We know a way, though. Do you know how to get to the main fishing port? There is a secret tunnel that leads from there right into the Southern Quarter. We were trying to get there when we got picked up. We'd got ourselves completely lost.'

Petruvio smiled again. 'How strange that you should say that. Because of how much I hate working for my uncle, I've been wanting to leave his service and become a simple fisherman. It is the only way he might willingly let me go. I have been going to the fishing port regularly. It's due south-west of here. Look, we really must leave right away. The longer we stay here the more chance there'll be of them finding you gone and coming after us.'

The three fugitives found an unattended boat on the canal that headed south and began their journey, switching canals every now and again when they saw patrols ahead. For Polly and Lisa the suspense was almost unbearable. They knew that if they were caught again, there would be no question as to their fate – Solon would have them executed instantly. On the plus side, Petruvio was probably the most skilled boatman they had ever come across. With the length of rope used to tie up the boat, he could lasso the posts that were placed along the edges of the canal and bring the boat to an almost instant halt. This he did many times, in order to slip over the side and swim ahead underwater to check what lay around the bends.

It was all going according to plan and eventually they could see that they were approaching the wall of the dome and therefore the fishing port. It was then that Petruvio, feeling relieved to have almost reached their destination, slipped up, carelessly failing to check the last bend. They sailed straight into a blockade.

Polly and Lisa's hearts plummeted and they both shook uncontrollably, unable to utter a word. Before Petruvio could do anything, another patrol boat appeared, hemming them in from behind. Without hesitating, Petruvio leaped on to the deck of one of the crafts. He appeared furious. 'Don't you know who I am?' he screamed at the startled guards.

The leading officer seemed apprehensive. He knew only too well how senior Petruvio was in Solon's administration. 'Of course, sir, but you are with the two girls who were arrested last night.'

'Well, I'm well aware of that, you stupid fool. They are under my custody – can't you see? I am taking them for interrogation on Solon's orders. Now, do you want me to take your name and rank? I could make life very difficult for you.'

The man looked nervous. 'N-no, my lord,' he stuttered. 'I was only doing my job.'

At the mention of 'my lord', Polly and Lisa couldn't help themselves and tried to stifle a snigger.

'Well, get on with your job,' Petruvio continued, 'and leave me to get on with mine. I'm on very serious business – do you understand?'

'I was only —'

Petruvio raised his hand to quieten him. 'Be on your way, before I lose my temper completely. '

The guard looked at him, trying to comprehend why Petruvio seemed to be taking the girls away from the city, but in the end his fear got the better of him. The two boats sped away, leaving Petruvio, Polly and Lisa to carry on their journey.

'From now on,' said Petruvio, 'I think you had better

lie flat in the bottom of the boat. I'm sure that once they have reported back to command they'll be straight after us again. We have very little time.'

And so it was. Just as they were approaching the quayside, they heard the roar of boats behind them. Without hesitating, Petruvio dived over the side of the canal into a smaller one which was passing underneath. Polly and Lisa followed and swam as fast as they had ever swum before, in pursuit of their new and highly unlikely saviour.

Chapter 12

THOROUGHLY EXHAUSTED FROM the tension, Matt and Lydia had slept soundly on the cold floor of the windowless cell they shared with the rest of the prisoners in Room 37. They were woken after what seemed just a few hours by the sound of a key turning in the lock and the guard rapping hard on the studded metal door.

'What happens now?' whispered Matt to the man next to him.

'We go to work, of course. It's nearly dark-time again. It's all we ever do. Work, sleep and then work again. Every day is the same.'

'Where? Where do we work?'

'For the last few weeks, all the men from this corridor have been put to work in the munitions factory, making weapons and ammunition. The women remain in the fields.'

'Why are they making more weapons?'

'We don't know, but we thought that something big might be going on above.'

Matt thought of the Polizia surrounding the Southern Quarter and shuddered.

The door swung open and a burly guard carrying a large gun and a whip ordered them to line up outside. He lashed out at a couple of the prisoners who he thought weren't moving fast enough, causing them to stumble and fall to their knees. Matt and Lydia kept their heads down as they passed, praying that he wouldn't notice that they were intruders.

Without a word spoken, they shuffled along with the others into the great hall and on to the train which was to take them first to the distribution centre and from there to their various work destinations. The men and women were to be separated at this point. Matt and Lydia hesitated. They had planned to stay together at all costs and now they were to be pulled apart. Lydia, who was not given to any show of emotion, put her hands to her eyes to hide her tears. She had grown to love her new brother in the short time she had known him. After a poignant goodbye, Matt went with the men to another staircase that led up to a huge, windowless hall, full of machinery. Steam and smoke filled the air and the noise of massive steam hammers and drills was almost enough to split the poor surfer's eardrums.

Matt was taken with about thirty other men to the forge, where weapons were created to arm the Polizia. Lines of filthy, sweating labourers, stripped to the waist, worked the roaring furnaces. The temperature was almost unbearable and poor Matt, though much fitter than the rest of the workforce, wondered whether he'd be able to cope. One man soon collapsed prostrate on the floor. After a couple of minutes, he was dragged unceremoniously out of the room by sniggering guards. Matt could only guess his fate.

After several hours, the exhausted workers were allowed to leave the room and rest for a short while, not due to sudden feelings of compassion on the guards' behalf, but so they could get the greatest amount of work possible out of them. Matt could hardly think straight and lay on his back, desperately trying to get the slightly cooler air into his lungs. Had he been mad to come to Devilla?

Glancing around, he saw batches of extremely vicious looking weapons being taken to the store room. If the Polizia were about to arm themselves with these, Matt thought, the consequences for the rebels would be very serious indeed. He could only pray that the Southern Quarter rebellion would happen before they could be distributed.

He'd only been there a short time when he was tapped gently on the shoulder. A youngish man, with a face much older than his years, spoke quietly to him. 'Word has gone around that you were one of the children that was sent to the surface many years ago.'

'That's true,' whispered Matt. 'We have only just returned.'

The man continued. 'I can't speak for long, but one of the men in my neighbouring work unit lost both his children when they were babies. They were twins. One was a girl who stayed in Fortuna and the other was a boy who was taken up by the woman of the Southern Quarter.'

Matt was astonished. 'Where is this man?' he asked, suddenly forgetting how drained he felt.

'His name is Lorca and he is over in the area where they make explosives.'

Matt jumped to his feet almost as if he'd had an electric shock. He was almost certain it was the name that Lydia had mentioned when they first realised that they were brother and sister. 'I have to see him,' he said urgently. 'He might be my father.'

'He will be over by the largest steam hammer when you have your next break. You might see him then. I must go – the guard is coming back this way.'

Matt could hardly bear the excitement at the prospect of meeting his real father – and so uncannily quickly. As soon as the siren signalled their next break, he dashed over to where the massive hammer had ground to a halt. The guards were all in a bunch talking, and the exhausted workers were lying on the ground resting . . . all except one. One of the older-looking men had remained on his feet. The two walked towards each other silently and stood for a long time, searching each other's faces.

'Do you know your number?' the man asked, almost suspiciously.

'It's fourteen,' said Matt in a quiet voice.

The older man said nothing, but tears began to run down his face, making streaks in the grime. His bottom lip trembled. 'And your name?'

'My name on the surface has been Matthew – but apparently, so my sister told me, my given name was Antonio.'

The man walked forward, hesitated and put his hands on Matt's shoulders.

Slightly embarrassed, Matt looked into his eyes. 'Are you my father?'

'My name is Lorca. Your mother's name is Celina.'

'Is she still . . . ?' Matt tried to ask.

'Yes, she is still alive, but only just. She is extremely unwell. Unless she gets some proper rest, she will surely be dead within weeks – either by natural causes or termination.'

'I have to see her!' cried Matt.

The man lowered his voice to a whisper. 'Maybe

there will be a chance tonight when we go back to eat. Why are you here? How did they catch you?'

'They didn't. Your daughter Lydia – my twin sister – and I came here yesterday of our own accord.'

Lorca's eyes widened. 'Are you mad? Why would you do a thing like that?'

'I think you might know the reason. We came to find you and my mother and to help you and the other prisoners get away from here.'

His expression collapsed. 'I am afraid you are deluded, my boy. There is no escape from this ghastly life. We are resigned to it. Please don't bring your false hopes here.'

'Then you haven't heard?'

Lorca was puzzled and looked round to make sure the guards were still occupied.

'There is to be a huge rebellion in a few days' time throughout Fortuna,' explained Matt. 'It has been organised by the elders of the Southern Quarter. The plan is to overthrow Solon and set everyone free. We are here to let you all know so that you can at least be ready.'

'But how? We are weak and have no weapons.'

'No weapons? But you are working in an arms factory!'

A strange look came into Matt's father's face. His tired eyes began to widen and his eyebrows lifted. It was an unmistakable look of hope. He turned around furtively to check again that nobody was listening. 'You're not suggesting . . . ?'

'There are maybe three hundred men here and only ten or so guards on any one shift. If everyone rose up at precisely the same moment they wouldn't stand a chance — especially if we could break into the arms store.'

The old man smiled grimly. 'We wouldn't have to do that. We are made to take the finished weapons in and out of there. It is never locked.'

'Why have you not thought of that before?'

'There was an attempt some time back. Three men came out of the armoury firing. Not only were they gunned down on the spot, but ten others were terminated as a lesson to anyone else who might have the same idea.'

At that point the steam-hammer began its ferocious din again and any more conversation became impossible. One of the returning guards had seen them talking and whacked Matt full in the stomach with the butt of his gun, taking his breath away. Matt, having always been quite a physical person and not averse to defending himself, raised his hand to strike back, but his father, spotting this immediately, grabbed both his arms just before he was able to act further. The guard stood there laughing, but Matt could tell he was slightly puzzled —

this was possibly the only sign of resistance he had ever witnessed.

Lorca smiled grimly. 'I am proud to be your father. I hope I will prove worthy of you.'

Matt looked serious. 'Oh no, Father. I only hope I will one day feel worthy of the sacrifice you and my mother have made for me.'

Matt continued the back-breaking work for the rest of the day and met Lydia back in the great food hall.

'They're alive – both them,' he whispered excitedly, forgetting the pain. 'I met our father. He is well, just about – but our mother is very sick, apparently.'

'That is amazing! Was he excited to see you?'

'He couldn't believe we'd come here. He thought we were insane. He said we might see him here.'

Lydia looked round the crowded hall despairingly. 'How will we ever find him?'

'You stay right here and I'll go and search.'

Despite aching all over and being practically delirious with exhaustion, Matt began to search the hall for his father. After about half an hour he realised that he had to get some food and returned to fetch Lydia. As they joined the end of the queue, Matt heard the name 'Antonio' being called in a barely audible voice. He turned to see his father sitting at a table nearby and cradling a woman's head in his lap, trying to spoon-feed her from his bowl. Luckily the nearest guard had been called over to a disturbance near the food-serving area. One of the prisoners had stolen an extra piece of bread and had been dragged away screaming.

Lydia and her brother went over to them and fell to their knees. They had found their parents at last.

Chapter 13

THE TUNNEL TO THE fishing port had become a constant thoroughfare as the small groups who were circulating news of the planned rebellion came and went from the Southern Quarter. The atmosphere was almost electric as everyone realised the enormity of what was planned. There were reports that news of the rebellion was spreading like wildfire.

The main hall of the Southern Quarter had become a centre of operations and teams of elders grouped together to concentrate on the specific areas that they would attack when the time came.

Those developing weapons had been working constantly and they were proud to announce that soon anyone who could possibly use a weapon in the fight ahead – man, woman or child – could have one. The plan was to overpower the guards at the entrance of

Devilla and storm the place as soon as the rebellion started. It was hoped also, of course, that Matt and Lydia would have prepared everyone there – providing their cover hadn't already been blown – so the Devillans there could assist them.

Petruvio was arrested immediately on his arrival with Polly and Lisa in the Southern Quarter, since he was near the top of the enemy wanted list. He had been well aware this would happen and explained to his captors that although he had been groomed to be the dreaded Solon's right-hand man, he had come to realise what a tyrant Solon was. Gradually, as he revealed more and more information, his interrogators became convinced he genuinely wanted to help them and that he could be extremely useful to their cause.

'Because of the urgency of the situation,' Theron announced, after Petruvio had been interrogated for many hours, 'we have decided to trust you. If you are lying to us, then you will be sorry.'

Petruvio stood tall. 'I have not lied to you, I give you my word. Despite what you may think of me, I am an honest man. I may have been deluded, but I am honest. Perhaps my main sin has been naivety.'

'Well,' said Theron, with a grim smile, 'if you really have joined us, we can make tremendous use of you. I presume you have a good knowledge of your uncle's palace. I believe it is more like a fortress.'

'I know it like the back of my hand. I was brought up there from a tiny child and know every corridor and every room.'

'Would you be prepared to lead a party to capture Solon?'

'I would be honoured. But I warn you, the palace is always heavily guarded. There is only one secret way in that I know of, but it is tricky. It is the one I used to get the girls out of the dungeon. I only hope it hasn't been discovered.'

'How many men will you need?'

'No more than one. We must attract as little attention as possible. If we can get to my uncle's state rooms before we are intercepted, we can take him hostage. But time is of the essence. He comes from a long line of cowards and liars and he will do anything to avoid being hurt, let alone killed.'

'Then you will choose one of our strongest and cleverest young men to accompany you.'

'It would be wise if he knew exactly how the Southern Quarter operates. If we are to work together we must learn from each other's strengths,' concluded Petruvio.

That evening Polly and Lisa sat with Petruvio and began to tell him all about the world above – all the things he had seemed to refuse to acknowledge before.

'You must have thought me very stupid for not listening to you or asking questions when you were last here,' he said sadly. 'I just didn't want to believe the rumours and I was under strict orders not to talk to you about anything like that. I was being constantly watched.'

'We didn't understand what a hold that old monster had on everyone,' said Lisa. 'There were times we wanted to shake you – but then we became afraid of you.'

'Afraid?'

'Afraid you might snitch on us.'

'Snitch?'

'Sorry, that means telling stories to get people into trouble.'

'I never actually did that. And when I found out that I myself was under surveillance by one of Solon's men, I had to deal with him . . . permanently.'

Both girls realised together that beneath Petruvio's rather gentle outer appearance was an extremely strong and ruthless streak that could be switched on at a moment's notice. That didn't stop Lisa fancying him like mad, of course – but then she always had.

'Are you afraid?' Polly asked their rescuer.

'I can't afford to be afraid. When I think of my uncle, I become so angry I could tear him apart with my own bare hands.' As if to make his point, Petruvio clenched his fist and pounded it into his other hand. He looked so angry that for a second it seemed as if he would burst a blood vessel. 'By not telling me the real truth behind Fortuna, he has deceived me every day of my life – and he must pay.'

'Who did *you* think did all the work in Fortuna? Where did you imagine your food came from, for instance?' asked Lisa.

Petruvio gave the impression that he wished he could sink right through the floor. 'I am so ashamed. I knew that someone must have had to do it, but we were taught never to ask questions, even as little children. Our parents never said anything and we were punished if we mentioned such things. It was like a huge conspiracy. After a while it was easier not to think about it – so we didn't.'

'And who did you think maintained the power to heat the dome and provide the air to breathe?' Lisa persisted, beginning to look cross.

'We believed it just sort of happened. If we ever asked, we were told not to. It is no excuse, I know, but that was how it was.'

'And who did you think made your clothes and the little boats you sailed around in?' Lisa was like a dog with a bone, refusing to give up.

'They were just there – whenever we wanted them.'

'How extremely convenient, eh, Polly? They could

even have been made by our poor mothers and fathers in Devilla.'

Petruvio stared into the girls' eyes, turned away and put his head in his hands. To their huge surprise his broad shoulders began to shake uncontrollably and he suddenly burst into loud sobs. It was the first time Polly and Lisa had seen anyone cry in Fortuna.

'Let's just hope you will get the chance to make it up to them,' said Lisa, in a slightly kinder voice.

Petruvio looked up like a wild animal and jumped to his feet. 'If they are alive I will find them, I promise. It will be my task in life . . . after I have brought down Solon and all he stands for.'

Chapter 14

BACK IN THE HUGE feeding hall, Matt and Lydia leaned over their mother, Celina, who stared up at them, her pale green, sunken eyes wild with wonder. 'Is it really you?' she murmured. 'Are you really my beautiful children come back to me? It must be a miracle.'

Lydia could hardly speak with emotion, but eventually found her voice. 'Yes, Mother, it is us,' she replied quietly. 'Here is your son, Antonio, whom you have not seen since he was a few weeks old. He has come from the surface to rescue you and Father and all the other poor people of Devilla.'

'I feel it may be too late for me. I do not think I can last much longer. If I cannot go back to work soon I will be of no use to them and they will terminate me. But that is of no consequence now.'

Lydia grasped her hand. 'Please try to keep going

just a bit longer; in a matter of days it will all be over and you will be free.'

Matt and Lydia's father bent over her again. 'You must take some food, my dear, it is the only way you will survive.'

With a little more coaxing, the poor woman took some of the tepid broth into her mouth and then a faint look of hope came into her face, just as it had with her husband earlier. 'My little Lydia, you are so beautiful – and Antonio, what a fine, strong man you are. I have thought of you every single day. You are right, I must try to —'

But her husband had just seen the guard returning to his position and put his hand gently over her mouth. The guard would have beaten them if he had seen them talking.

At that point the siren wailed to tell them it was time to make their way to their rooms to sleep. Matt and Lydia hugged their mother and father and swore that they would try to see them every day until the rebellion began. As they joined the sad queue, they looked back to see their mother rising shakily to her feet stumbling forward with new life.

As Matt and Lydia shuffled along, they couldn't help noticing that just about everyone was now staring at them. So obvious was it to them that they became worried in case the guards might notice. The word had obviously spread like flames across a dry prairie, for there was an intense glint of determination in the haggard faces of the prisoners that they hadn't noticed before.

When they were safely locked in their room, the others gathered round excitedly. The woman who had first spoken to them began. 'The word has gone round. We all now know that something enormous is about to happen. Unfortunately there are spies amongst us who report on disturbances in order to get extra food and privileges. When you have nothing and are continually on the verge of starvation, you notice those who are surviving better than you are. We have all known about them and who they are for a long, long time and they have now been warned that if they go to the guards, they will be the first to be dealt with by us as soon as the rebellion starts. They appear to have heeded our words. For the very first time these spies are more scared of us than the guards.'

Matt smiled grimly. 'You must tell everyone to make their way straight to the arms factory when the battle begins. I will organise for everyone to be supplied with weapons by those who work there. They have a huge store of guns and rifles which are ready to go to the army that is about to invade the Southern Quarter. We can only hope they don't attack first. When you get there, you should be joined by those of the Southern Quarter whose job it will be to storm the entrance.'

'Where will we go if we manage to escape?' asked a woman from the back of the room.

'There will be people there to help you. The most important thing will be not to panic.'

'We will not do that,' said an older man. 'It is worth risking our lives for the chance to escape this terrible place.'

A chorus of agreement filled the room.

'Then all we can do is wait,' said Lydia, '. . . and pray.'

Chapter 15

*T*HEY DIDN'T HAVE TO wait long. Everyone in the Southern Quarter had been well aware that the chances of Solon and his henchmen *not* receiving news of the rebellion were fairly remote. Reports had come to the old man that his own nephew had rescued the two girls and it had rendered him incandescent with rage. Petruvio had kept his dissatisfaction with the regime very secret, until now.

So many people had been spreading the word around Fortuna, that it was a small miracle that Solon hadn't heard about the proposed rebellion earlier. It was the father of the angry boy to whom Polly and Lisa had spoken who finally raised the alarm. This man was one of the senior officers in Solon's guard and when his son told him of his encounter with the girls, he informed Solon immediately.

'It is nothing. They can never defeat us. But let us attack them before they launch their pathetic attack on us,' the Imperial Governor responded.

As the lights went down that night, Solon's men began mounting an attack on the north side of the Southern Quarter. Theron realised that they must retaliate immediately, and he ordered a heavily armed division to meet the attackers. The battle had begun!

To say the Polizia were surprised at the rebels' response was an understatement. They had expected some resistance, but nothing compared to the amazing new weapons that practically sent their boats flying out of the water. After a couple of hours, they were forced to retreat in order to re-examine their strategy, allowing hundreds of the rebels from the Southern Quarter to make their way north.

When Solon heard this, he summoned his most senior officers of the Polizia and palace guard to his state room. 'Are you really telling me they were able to hold us off?' he bellowed, his face twisted with fury. 'You drivelling fools. Why do we have spies? They should have been telling you about the resistance.'

'I think they must have been captured, your lordship,' one of them replied. 'Or maybe they're all double agents and actually working *for* the opposition. They told us that the rebels only had a few of the ancient weapons left over from when they first broke away. We can only suppose they must have been manufacturing these new arms. Some of their weapons seemed more powerful than ours and almost silent. We can't even be sure how many people there are living in the Southern Quarter and fighting in Theron's army. I fear there might be many more than we thought.'

Solon was livid and waved his arms in the air furiously. 'So we have an enemy we don't know the size of, with powerful weapons we didn't know they had. This is ridiculous. We must attack on all fronts. They cannot defend every side – it is impossible!'

At that moment a huge explosion rocked the palace to its very foundations. Solon strode as fast as his old legs would carry him to the window, where he observed a growing pall of black smoke in the distance. 'I don't believe it. It looks as if they've blown up the main canal going south! Do you realise what this means? They're not just content to defend their own – they're starting to fight back. Maybe there is more to this rebellion than we thought.'

Solon's generals looked genuinely shocked. They too had supposed that the talk of a full-scale rebellion was an exaggeration, and were regretting not taking it more seriously.

Chapter 16

MATT HAD BEEN SLAVING AWAY in the arms factory for a few days. Although tired and continually hungry, he was beginning to get used to the hard work and felt reasonably strong and more than ready for the fight ahead. He was just returning from his first break when he saw two of the guards in urgent conversation. He sidled up alongside them and overheard them saying that the main canal had been blown up by rebels. Matt realised that the rebellion had begun and that it was his job and his alone to rally the men. He did not have to do very much to get their attention, as for some time they had been watching him and waiting for a signal. He lifted his arms and the machinery ground to a halt.

Matt leaped onto one of the silent forges and yelled at the top of his voice. 'Men of Devilla, the time for battle has come. Run to the armoury and grab your weapons right away. You must now fight for your own freedom.'

At that moment a shot rang out and Matt felt a stinging sensation at the top of his left arm, but before the guard who had shot him could aim again, he was overwhelmed by a mob of angry workers. More guards poured in, responding to the shouts of the Devillans, but the first of the workers had reached the armoury and began the retaliation, with the other workers soon joining them. Most were unarmed and not physically strong, but by their sheer number and with a blind, ter-rifying fury that had taken years to accumulate, they managed to overpower the guards who, after a token resistance, fled in terror or surrendered.

Now heavily armed, Matt and his fellow workers stormed out to liberate the whole of Devilla, realising that the impossible might just be possible after all.

Chapter 17

PETRUVIO CHOSE A YOUNG MAN called Darius to accompany him on his dangerous mission to capture Solon. Darius was not only exceptionally brave, but a favourite of Theron's, and was one of the major planners of the rebellion. His knowledge of the inner workings of Fortuna, and especially the Southern Quarter, was better than anyone's, which made him a natural choice.

To Theron, the capture of Solon and his removal from power was probably the most important part of their plan. Being someone who hated violence, Theron believed that taking Solon as a prisoner, rather than killing him, would set a fine example for the future.

Petruvio and Darius had practically no time to discuss their strategy. They decided they would rely on Petruvio's knowledge of his uncle's palace to get them to Solon. Once they had caught him, they would smuggle him out of the palace the way they had come, take him to the Southern Quarter and make him surrender publicly. Surely this would signal victory for the rebels.

Polly and Lisa were there to see Petruvio and Darius off. 'We wish you luck,' said Polly. 'Solon is terrifying – but there's no better man to challenge him finally than you.'

Petruvio smiled grimly. 'I can't think what he'll do when he sees me, but I don't think he'll be inviting me to dine with him.'

The girls giggled nervously and, as they did so, realised it was the first joke they had ever heard Petruvio make. He, in turn, laughed with them, as he too realised what he had just done. Lisa then ran forward and kissed him full on the lips, leaving him looking slightly dazed.

As Darius led Petruvio through the tunnel that led to the fishing port, they came across many excited people who had been to collect their weapons for the fight ahead.

Once they emerged from the tunnel, at the fishing port, Petruvio and his companion had no choice but to travel overground, and their journey became more difficult. Small skirmishes were breaking out everywhere. There were now a number of Fortunans from outside the Southern Quarter, who were joining the rebels – many of them young people who had only recently been told the truth about the murderous Solon and his dreaded Polizia.

Just about every canal was now blocked and Petruvio and Darius were anxious to avoid a fight. The whole journey was like making their way through an enormous maze, with the young men often having to travel in the opposite direction to where they were heading in order to circumnavigate the various obstacles. Being forced to change canals every few minutes made their progress terribly slow, but eventually Petruvio got them to the small pool in the square that led to the underground lift-shaft.

Once inside, it was Petruvio's childhood knowledge of the palace that came into its own. Interwoven between the numerous grand hallways and internal courtyards were hundreds of narrow, secret passageways that the 'invisible' army of slave servants used in order to service the rich palace dwellers. Petruvio had never seen these people, as they only ever operated in the middle of the dark-time, but as a child he had often played in the passageways during the daytime, even though they were supposed to be out of bounds.

Darius felt rather confused as Petruvio led him through the labyrinth of corridors and staircases. At times he thought they must be going round in circles but his partner seemed to know exactly where he was and led them eventually to a small door, where he stopped to catch his breath.

'If I've got it right, Solon's chambers are on the other side of this door,' he whispered. 'It's always locked when he is inside.'

Darius smiled. 'I know how to pick locks. My father used to make clock and gun mechanisms. I always carry little pieces of wire with me, just in case.'

Petruvio was pleased and slapped his new friend on the shoulder. He put his ear to the small door, and could hear the sound of footsteps. 'It's my uncle – he always walks around when he's thinking hard. I can't hear anyone else, so we must strike now, while he is alone.'

Solon was pacing up and down beside his huge window. He was still convinced his army would quell the rebellion. He was angry that the rebels were so much better prepared than he thought, but there were several other aspects to this conflict that worried him. Most of all, he hated the idea of Petruvio being on the loose. His nephew's knowledge of the palace and the workings of the city were second to none, so all the time he was free he was a severe threat.

As Solon paced up and down, he was sure he could hear a metallic clinking noise in the room but, try as he might, he couldn't work out what it was or where it was coming from.

On the other side of the door, Darius had found it far harder to pick the lock than he had anticipated. Petruvio searched his colleague's face as he worked patiently in the semi-darkness, hoping to see signs of a breakthrough. He held his weapon in his hand, ready for the moment the door opened. Eventually there was a loud click and the door began to swing inwards. Petruvio and Darius looked up . . . to meet Solon's gaze.

'So it is you!' sneered the old man, staring into the barrels of the two guns.

Chapter 18

AT THAT MOMENT, the Imperial Governor's personal guards burst through the door at the far side of the chamber. The guards, seeing their master in such a delicate position, skidded to a halt with their guns pointed at the two intruders.

'I think you would be wise not to use those,' Petruvio yelled at them. 'Your master would be hit before us.'

Solon looked positively frightened. He turned to face the guards. 'Put down your weapons. I must talk with my nephew.'

Petruvio and Darius stood for several minutes with their guns trained on Solon. Looking at him, Darius soon realised that their plan to capture Solon and take him back the way they had come could never have worked – he was just too old and fragile for the journey. Darius had no idea what to do. Could they force Solon to gather all his generals together and order them to stop the fighting?

Solon relaxed his angular body and turned to face his nephew. 'Petruvio, my dear boy,' he crooned in a soft, syrupy voice. 'What has happened to set you against your beloved uncle? Haven't I always given you everything you ever desired?'

Petruvio let out a mocking laugh. 'I cannot deny that, Uncle, but you are old and cannot to be trusted any more.'

'But to join the rebels . . . Why would you do such a thing?'

'You make too many assumptions, Uncle.'

At this remark, Darius eyed Petruvio curiously.

Solon continued. 'But you helped those girls escape from my dungeons.'

'Things aren't always what they seem.'

Darius was now staring hard at Petruvio, trying to understand what he was saying.

At that moment, a hoard of heavily-armed Polizia broke into the huge room and saw the weapons trained on Solon.

'Put down your guns,' barked Solon, realising how fragile the situation had become.

The leader of the Polizia did nothing but seemed to be watching Petruvio, as if waiting for a signal.

'Did you not understand me?' Solon screamed. 'I will be killed if you shoot.'

Petruvio turned to the man, smiled and inclined his head slightly. At this, the leader of the Polizia lifted his gun slowly, took aim . . . and shot Solon right between the eyes.

Petruvio stared down at the body of his dead uncle and laughed. Darius, on the other hand, was deeply shocked. This was not part of the plan. Theron had ordered them to capture Solon alive, but he was now dead at their feet. Darius turned to Petruvio, only to see that his gun was now pointing at him.

'What are you doing?' he cried. 'Have you gone crazy?'

'What do you think I'm doing?' snarled Petruvio, with a cruel smile. 'Lower your weapon. I have just got rid of the only person in my way to becoming the Imperial Governor of Fortuna. This old man was not capable of fighting a rebellion; his time was over.'

Darius looked across to the Polizia who were all smiling and pointing their weapons at him and Solon's personal guards, who now looked dumbfounded and confused.

Petruvio turned to Darius. 'For some time now I have been the head of the secret division of the Polizia.'

As Darius looked straight into Petruvio's eyes, the full implications of what had happened dawned on him. 'So you simply used the two young girls to get into the Southern Quarter.'

'Well done, Darius,' he replied sarcastically. 'It worked well, didn't it? Especially the way I persuaded your foolish leader, Theron, that I was to be trusted.'

Darius looked even more confused. 'So why did you want me to come along with you?'

'You are so stupid. You have an intimate knowledge of the Southern Quarter and its strong and weak points. You will head the main attack as my hostage. We will hold you in front of us. If Theron's men shoot at us he will have to kill you first.'

Darius laughed dryly. 'You will never get into the Southern Quarter.'

It was Petruvio's turn to laugh. 'Oh, I rather think, with a little help from you, we might.'

Darius's mind raced. 'I will never tell you anything,' he scowled.

'Oh yes you will,' said Petruvio with a smirk. 'We have methods that make anything Solon did seem gentle. You will be begging to tell us everything by the time we have finished with you.' He turned to his guards. 'Now, take him below.'

Chapter 19

ALTHOUGH NO ONE YET knew of Solon's death, the word was all over Fortuna that Devilla had been liberated. The canals were full of excited citizens making their way towards the prison to see what could be done for the former inmates. Polly and Lisa realised that this was the chance they had been waiting for to see if their parents were still alive, and joined the crowds.

When they finally arrived at Devilla, the sight that greeted their eyes took their breath away. Instead of just a group of deserted buildings in a barren compound, hundreds people were milling around, cheering, many of them greeting long-lost relatives. Inside the main hall, the scene was the same and the two girls spotted Matt and Lydia on the platform where the food had once been distributed. Pushing through the ecstatic crowd, they finally joined them in a tearful reunion.

Polly and Lisa's eyes ran backwards and forwards over the happy faces, wondering if their parents could possibly be amongst them. Among the faces they glimpsed was the gorgeous Balia, their previous guide in the Southern Quarter, who gave them a smile as they caught his eye.

Lydia cleared her throat and in a strong, confident voice addressed the crowd, who went silent almost immediately. 'You are probably wondering,' she cried, 'who these new girls are. They are from the land above the sea and they came back with me and my brother to help rescue you from the evil regime. All three of them – Matt, Lisa and Polly – were born in Fortuna and each of them was sent to the surface by the wonderful lady, Maricia. Like me and my brother, Polly and Lisa have also come back to see what has become of their long lost parents. Some of you will know that all the rescued babies were given numbers and that these were put on their backs before they were taken to the surface. Polly here was number seventeen.'

After a short hesitation, a high pitched scream came from the back of the hall, followed by a loud commotion. Everyone turned to see a woman pushing her way frantically through the mass of bodies to the front. Polly stood on tiptoes, trying to get a better view. Gradually, as the crowd parted, a tall, desperately thin woman broke through to the front, with tears streaming down her ravaged, but obviously once beautiful, face.

'Theodora!' she cried. 'Is it really you? I can't believe it, my daughter is alive! I just cannot believe it.'

Polly leaped off the stage and into the frail woman's open arms. Seeing them together, there was absolutely no doubt that Polly was her long lost daughter.

'My name is Oliviera. Your father died several years ago,' she said quietly, then looked down at Polly and smiled. 'But he would have been so pleased to see what a wonderful young woman you have become.'

As they talked excitedly, no one could hear Lisa's high-pitched voice coming from the stage. 'I am number twenty-one,' she cried. 'My real name is Hortensia.'

But the crowd had resumed their celebrations, so she stood there, praying that someone would call out. She yelled out her number again and again, hardly able to bear the disappointment.

Matt and Lydia, noticing her distress, ran over to comfort her.

'It's not over yet,' cried Matt. 'There are still loads of people outside. They were defending the entrance when the Polizia tried to take Devilla back. Maybe your parents are amongst them.'

Chapter 20

POLLY AND HER MOTHER, Oliviera, hardly knew where to start. Once the fuss had died down, they moved to a quieter corner and sat gazing at each other in wonder.

'When did you first find out where you had come from?' Polly was asked, after a short while.

'It was an accident really. It only started when I discovered I could breathe underwater.' Then Polly quickly explained the chain of events that had led to her and her friend Lisa's accidental discovery of the lower ocean.

'How is that wonderful woman, Maricia, who sent you away? Is she still with us?'

'She is still alive but very old and very frail. We met her when we came down to Fortuna the first time.'

Oliviera's eyes opened wide. 'You have been down

before? You are so brave to come back. I have heard that the world up there above the water is truly wonderful.'

Polly smiled. 'You have no idea, living in this horrid place. I'll have time to tell you all about it when we are out of here. But what about you? How have you survived?'

'Sometimes it has only been the thought of you and the free life I hoped you would be living that kept me going. Many times I just wanted to crawl into a corner and die. I have been down here for fourteen years now and every day has seemed like a lifetime. We are all so terribly tired.'

'It will soon be over, Mother – er, can I call you Mother? It will soon be over and you will be able to rest then.'

That was it! Hearing her long-lost daughter calling her Mother was just too much for Oliviera and she wept profusely, but this time with pure joy.

'What was my father like?' asked Polly when the tears had subsided.

'He was a wonderful and brave man,' she said, trying to control her voice. 'He was terminated when they found out that he had managed to get you away. They might have killed me, but for some reason they sent me here instead. I have often wondered which would have been better. This has been no more than a living death.'

Polly suddenly flushed and looked furious. 'They will be made to pay for this,' she cried. 'The people of the Southern Quarter will see to it.'

Polly's mother looked sad. 'Why, my darling? Nothing will bring your father back or anyone else who perished here. Look, I have no anger. All I want is to live like a human being again. In a way, I am as guilty as anyone else. Until I was about to have you, I just carried on pretending everything was all right. People are very weak.'

'But didn't you wonder how everyone lived so well?'

'We had nothing to compare it with. That was how we lived and that was all that seemed to matter.'

'How long has Devilla been going?'

'Nobody really knows. There are people here whose parents were here before them, and their parents too. Sometimes, if a baby is born here, it is allowed to live, especially if the workforce is dropping. Mothers have to take them to work with them. The guards are all so cruel.'

'Do you know my friend Lisa's parents?'

'Possibly – I know several people who also sent their children away. But it has been difficult to talk down here. Tell me about Lisa.'

'She is much braver than me. She is my best friend. It's funny, we only really knew we were different when we met each other. If we hadn't met by pure chance, maybe this whole thing wouldn't have happened.'

They had only been talking for a few minutes when there was a huge commotion at the entrance to Devilla. A man, streaked in blood and dirt, burst through the crowds screaming at the top of his voice. 'It is over! It is finally over! We are completely free! Free, do you understand? The very last of the guards have thrown down their weapons. We have been saved by our brothers and sisters from the Southern Quarter and those Fortunans who have decided to oppose Solon.' He then collapsed with the emotion of it all.

The noise was indescribable. Men cheered, women cried and everyone milled around almost out of control. Poor Lisa, meanwhile, was still on the raised platform with Matt and Lydia, desperately calling out for her parents.

Among the people who had been fighting were a fierce-looking couple who were carried in at shoulder height. Everyone cheered and slapped them on the back.

Polly leaned over and spoke to her mother. 'Who are those people?'

'They are called Helena and Christos. They have tried to keep our spirits up all the time we have been here – most of the time in vain. They have always believed this rebellion would happen. Most of us laughed at them.'

'How did they come to be in Devilla?'

'Oh, they were just like me and your father – they

were caught sending their child to the surface. I don't know if it was a girl or a boy. They too were lucky not to be executed.'

It was if something exploded in Polly's brain and she fought her way through to the couple, who were still being congratulated by the excited crowds.

'What was the number of your daughter?' Polly yelled to them.

The woman turned and looked puzzled. She did not recognise the person that was asking the question. In the midst of her triumph she looked sad. 'She was twenty-one,' she said wearily. 'I will remember that number until I die. Why?'

'Because that is your daughter Hortensia, over there on the platform. She came with us from the surface.'

The woman and her husband strained their eyes and saw Lisa, who was still searching the faces of the crowd. There are some things only a mother could possibly know and Helena, without any warning, uttered a strange, high-pitched cry, like a wild animal in pain. She then flew to the stage like a woman possessed, knocking people out of the way as she went. When she arrived, swiftly followed by her husband, she stopped and stood in front of Lisa, shaking and panting.

'Are you my . . . ?' cried Lisa, hardly able to say the word.

The woman nodded silently, tears running down her face. 'And here is your father,' said the woman. 'We gave you the name Hortensia. Your number was twenty-one.'

Lisa leaned over to Polly and whispered, 'Now I know what it's like to be a prize in a raffle.' They both laughed for the first time for ages.

Chapter 21

Darius was dragged out of Solon's state room into the main corridor and then whisked along the grand canal that flowed right through the centre of the city to a black granite tower he had only ever seen from the outside. He had, however, always understood it to be the headquarters of the secret Polizia.

Darius was kicked and punched for the best part of an hour but refused to speak at all. He held out for as long as he could, but when the punishment began to get serious, he broke down dramatically. The two savage interrogators asked if he was now prepared to tell them what they wanted to know.

'All right, all right,' Darius cried. 'I don't know much but what I do know, I'll tell you – I promise. Just don't hurt me any more, I beg of you.' The tears rolled down the young man's cheeks and splashed on the floor, making a pathetic picture.

'Look,' he continued, his voice distorted by grief, 'I didn't want to do this in the first place. I was forced to come with Petruvio to kidnap Solon. They chose me because I know my way in and out of the Southern Quarter better than anyone else. I don't care who rules Fortuna.'

The shadowy interrogators seemed pleased that the young man had broken so quickly and sent for Petruvio, who was waiting upstairs.

Petruvio swaggered into the room and smiled at his former colleague's apparent distress. He spoke in a much softer voice than the others. 'So, Darius my friend, I am very pleased you have seen sense. As you know, I hate hurting people.' He smiled evilly to the others, who laughed. 'I am sorry I had to deceive you in such a way, but you have information I need. I am sure you understand. The Southern Quarter must be crushed immediately, and you are the man to help me do it.'

Darius hesitated and then shook his head, as if he realised he had no choice. 'I r-really don't know what you want from me,' he muttered. 'Y-you have been to the Southern Quarter, you already know how it works.'

Petruvio continued to smile, but his voice turned

icy. 'Better than that – I managed to get detailed plans out of that fool Theron. Now I need to get my best men deep into the heart of the Southern Quarter. I must strike right at the nerve centre of this rebellion – I must destroy Theron and the council. But I need to know the best way of getting my men and weapons there. I don't know the way through that tunnel from the fishing port to the middle of the Southern Quarter, but you do. You will show us.'

'I will take you to the entrance is, as long as you let me go.'

Petruvio had been a little surprised at how easily Darius had broken down and was extremely wary. Who better than Petruvio to know how to fool people about one's sincerity? Because of the way that *he* worked, he knew this sudden compliance could well be a trap, but he also knew if he and his men were to take Darius with them as hostage, he would hardly be likely to lead them to his own certain death.

'We will take you with us,' Petruvio proclaimed. 'If anything happens to us, you will perish too. Based on your recent pathetic performance, I would imagine this would not be particularly satisfactory to you.'

His two henchmen laughed again at their master's attempt at humour.

The following morning, a battalion of heavily armed

soldiers was lined up in the main hall of the sinister Polizia building. They were carrying an assortment of savage-looking weapons. Darius, though bruised and battered from his ordeal with the interrogators, was dragged out and presented again to Petruvio.

'So, you scum, take us to the entrance to the tunnel that leads into the Southern Quarter and show us the correct way through it!' Petruvio ordered.

Darius was led out of the Polizia's headquarters and forced to accompany his captors through the canals towards the Southern Port. Petruvio had now been briefed on how badly things were going against the rebels and realised that it was absolutely crucial for them to destroy the command in the Southern Quarter. At the sight of the vicious batallion, those few people who were still around melted away.

Silas's tunnel was an ingenious feat of building, which harboured a dreadful secret – and Darius knew this. As he led them through, he took a turning different to the usual one, though it looked the same to the untrained eye. This turning led a long way under the ground towards the centre of the Southern Quarter, but it pos-sessed a feature that made it deadly – under the floor were ingenious mechanical triggers. These points were marked by small and otherwise inconspicuous marks on the walls.

The thirteenth mark was the one that held the

deadly secret. As soon as its trigger was disturbed, a chain of events had been designed to send the rocky ceiling tumbling down, trapping anyone unfortunate enough to have travelled beyond it. There would be no escape from that point.

Darius was an extremely clever young man and had realised earlier that to try and hold out against his torturers would have not only been pointless but terribly painful. He had always told himself that if he was ever in that position he would utilise his skills as an actor and pretend to crack when things got rough. He was justifiably worried, however.

By leading Petruvio and the others up this turning he was leading them to a certain death. But unless he could think of a way of separating himself from Petruvio and his men, he too would die. The only consolation was that his sacrifice would contribute greatly to the success of the rebellion.

As they progressed along the tunnel, Darius counted off the checkpoints, one by one, every twenty or so metres. He hoped he hadn't missed any of them. Darius was well aware that the only weapon he had was surprise, but how, he wondered, could he best use it? He was situated towards the front of the column as they marched onwards, but was hemmed in by armed Polizia on all sides.

On and on they walked, until eventually, they

approached the thirteenth marker. Once the trigger was disturbed, Darius knew he only had about ten seconds before the ceiling collapsed. As they reached the marker, Darius suddenly did the most extraordinary thing. From his slumped and shuffling walk, he simply screamed at the top of his voice and, flailing his hand above his head like a madman, crashed back through the startled Polizia, who were taken completely by surprise. Just as Darius had broken clear, he heard a cracking noise as the trigger was sprung. Bullets from behind whistled over his head and ricocheted off the stone around him.

Then the rocks began to tumble from the roof, striking him on the shoulders and back. Just as he was thinking he had left it too late he dived to the ground with all his strength and curled himself into a ball. The noise was deafening as, behind him, he could hear a combination of large boulders tumbling from above and the screams of the men who had been chasing after him and who were now being buried alive.

Darius lay several minutes in the pitch dark as the choking dust began to settle. He then sat up gingerly and felt himself all over. He realised that, though his cuts and bruises had been added to substantially, no serious damage had been done. Behind him, however, was a solid wall of rock and the only sound he could now hear was his own heavy breathing. He stood shakily and, feeling his way along the walls, began to edge his way back to the entrance. He was alive!

Chapter 22

As THE INITIAL EUPHORIA died down, the inhabitants of Devilla made their way outside. Despite their poor condition, they were revelling in their first taste of freedom, whilst being fussed over by a team of physicians and greeted by the rest of the Fortunans, who had been arriving in their droves to see the truth. All the Polizia had now been rounded up and locked in the very cells that had previously been the inmates' dormitories. They were to stay there until it was decided what to do with them. Theron had picked a special squad to act as guards and they made sure that, as more and more of the Polizia were brought in, they were taken below.

Every now and again, a cry of joy would break out as someone came across a distant relative or long-lost friend. Almost every family had at some time lost some-one to Devilla.

In the midst of all this, Theron climbed to the top of the watchtower, just a few metres from the ominous and sombre entrance to Devilla, and raised his hands. Most of the former inmates didn't know who he was, but his imposing appearance and commanding manner soon had them waiting in expectant silence.

'Brothers and sisters of Fortuna,' he began, 'this is probably the most significant day in the history of our land since the great flood. For those who don't know me already, my name is Theron, and when we have finally crushed Solon's evil regime, I will be in charge of the rebuilding of our society until proper elections can be held. Most of all, I must greet the prisoners of Devilla. For them particularly this must be the most momentous day of their lives. We can only guess what you all must have been forced to endure. All we can say is that we salute your bravery. Furthermore, we promise that if everything goes to plan your lives will be easy from now on. We plan a society where everyone will work for the good of others.'

Theron continued over the cheering. 'The most important thing now, we realise, is to get our poor brothers and sisters well again. As soon as everything is beginning to settle down, we will form a court and try those wicked people who made our lives so miserable. They will be punished accordingly but we will show more mercy than they ever showed their captives.

There has already been too much violence and misery in Fortuna.

'There are many people responsible for our victory. Some, who you might have heard about, have come from a land above the sea. These are the brave young people who risked their lives to return – not only to search for their parents, but to help overthrow Solon.

'We have witnessed some of the most heart-warming reunions. It is something I am sure that all concerned thought would never happen. Ahead we have a daunting task. To undo the work of Solon and replace it with a system requiring everyone to work for what they will receive will take a great deal of organisation. We will make mistakes, naturally, but we will strive towards a time when everyone's opinion will be heard and respected. In the meantime, we will use the Polizia to maintain the essential services. If they work hard and show signs of repentance they will eventually be freed to live like everybody else. We cannot any more have a society that feeds on cruelty. Most important of all, we will have a government that will be democratically elected by the people. If anyone becomes obsessed with power again, they will be voted out by all of us.

'I haven't really mentioned the land above the sea. A delegation from Fortuna will be sent to see what the situation really is up there. It has been said by the young people that have returned that the people there will be receptive to us and that eventually it might be possible for anyone to go there who desires to. The implications of this are fantastic, particularly where overcrowding is concerned. It means that no longer will people be forced into termination at sixty. I would beg you, however, not be too hasty in leaving. Fortuna can and will be the wonderful place it used to be before everything went so tragically wrong. We must all work together to make it so.'

Just as Theron was concluding his speech, a messenger arrived by boat, ran to the tower and shinned up the ladder to him. For some time the two men were locked in deep conversation. Theron then shook his head, smiled, turned to the crowd and punched the air triumphantly.

'People of Fortuna,' he cried, 'prepare yourselves for the news we have all been waiting for. The mighty Solon is no more. He has been slain by his own nephew, Petruvio. We are all now free to start a new life.'

The scenes below were indescribable as everyone embraced and cried for joy. Nobody would have been able to feel completely safe if the old tyrant had still been at large. Polly and Lisa, who were now near the front, jumped up and down and threw themselves at each other. They were so proud of Petruvio, the man who had saved their lives.

Theron silenced the crowd. 'As many of you from the

Southern Quarter might know, Petruvio, who had been primed to succeed Solon, came to us and convinced us that he had seen the error of his ways. He claimed that he wanted to be involved in our fight. We were all completely misled and I take full responsibility for this. I believed he would be an enormous asset to our cause. How wrong I have been.'

Polly and Lisa's smiles disappeared as they craned their heads to catch his every word.

'I am afraid he turned out be a true descendant of that wicked dynasty and was only using us for his own gain. Little did we know that he was the commander of the secret Polizia and that he planned to murder his uncle so that he could all the sooner claim his position as lord and master of Fortuna. He was also using the unrest as a tool to further his aims. His plan was to come back after killing Solon and strike deep into the heart of the Southern Quarter. Thanks to Darius, our faithful servant and now hero of all Fortuna, he is no longer a threat, being buried deep under the Southern Quarter with a battalion of his men.'

Polly and Lisa stared at each other in complete disbelief. They had been completely taken in by a man who, it now appeared, had simply used them.

Lisa was devastated and what had been tears of joy turned into sobs. 'But don't you remember how he broke down and everything? He begged us to forgive him. I really believed him. How could anyone be such a liar? I feel so stupid, Poll. He didn't care for us at all, he just wanted us to get him into the Southern Quarter.'

Polly put her arm round her friend. 'He was just like Solon. He simply trod on people to get what he wanted. Look, there's another way of seeing this. If that creep hadn't chosen to take us from Solon's dungeon, we could now be dead. We may have been just playing a part in his plan, but he probably saved our lives.'

Those of the Southern Quarter who had been unable to fight had, on hearing of the success of the rebellion prepared food for the occasion, and a vast feast was laid out for all to enjoy. Many of the poor prisoners, who had been forced to survive on minimum rations for so long, could hardly cope with the rich dishes that were laid out for them, much as they tried. But this could not dampen their joy at being liberated, and they relished every mouthful that they were able to eat.

Chapter 23

LIFE IN FORTUNA began to change rapidly. A decision was made to refurbish the buildings and canals of the Southern Quarter so that the whole place could return to its former splendour. A form of parliament was set up to decide, amongst other things, how the population might best be set to work. This work, whichever form it took, was to be rewarded with money or tokens, as it had been before Solon's cruel dynasty. As expected, many of the older Fortunans were set in their ways and resented having to do anything, but they soon learned that if they didn't work, they didn't eat – it was as simple as that.

Most of the younger population welcomed the new regime. It had to be said that life as one of the more fortunate Fortunans had become extremely tedious, with the majority having nothing to do from one day to the next. Indeed, most had never learned any practical skills whatsoever and had to be taught to do the most basic things for themselves. Fortunately, the only people who knew how to do anything were the former prisoners of Devilla, and this gave them a whole new status which helped greatly in their integration into Fortunan society.

As the Fortunans adapted to their new lives, the young people from the surface felt it was time to make up their minds where they wanted to live. Polly had grown very close to her mother, but she also knew that her real home would always be in England.

Lisa agreed. Much as she had been thrilled to meet her real mother and father, the idea of staying with them in this strange land under the ocean just didn't feel right to her. Like Polly, she decided to return to the surface but visit Fortuna whenever she could. The most important thing for both of them was that their real parents were now free to live happily for the rest of their lives in the knowledge that their daughters were safe and happy. It was now time for them to return to their adoptive parents.

Matt had known, almost from the start, that he would make his home in Fortuna with his sister. He realised his skills for organisation and leadership would be of far more use there and Theron was already talking of important jobs for him to do and he intended to try and find Kelly's parents too. He promised he would take Lydia to the surface again as soon as possible, however, and show her all the wonderful places in the world that he had visited. Their sick mother eventually began to show signs of a complete recovery and she and her husband were made very welcome in the Southern Quarter.

Only two days after the liberation of Fortuna, Maricia, who had turned out to be well over a hundred years old, died in her sleep, happy in the knowledge that Fortuna would be restored to its former glory.

And so it was that, on the eve of the first proper expedition back to the surface with representatives from Fortuna, the four friends met together to discuss the future once more.

'What have you all missed most being down here?' asked Lydia.

Lisa, as usual, spoke first. 'It's the size mostly. Being down here is like living in a small town and not ever being able to get out. I know I didn't travel much when I was on the surface, but I really like knowing there's a whole world to visit if you ever got the chance.'

'I miss all the different types of people,' said Polly. 'In our school alone we've got kids from all over the world.'

'I'll miss your bright sunshine and cold rain,' said Lydia. 'Everything down here is always the same – it's good, admittedly, but the same. Everyone seems to complain about the weather in England, but it is better than having none at all.'

'I know I'll miss surfing,' said Matt, 'but I suppose for a long time I've realised that balancing on a small board in the sea's not a proper job – not for ever. Being down here has taught me that I'm capable of so much more.'

'I think you'll be part of the council one day,' laughed Lydia. 'Theron thinks you're amazing.'

Matt laughed good-humouredly. 'That's *so* what I don't want. I'm far too lazy. I want to be able to go out and enjoy myself when I feel like it.'

'I think we'll all agree to that,' said Polly. 'How often do you think people will be able to go back and forth?'

'I reckon they'll be able to open up the passageway between the upper and lower oceans relatively soon. It could be almost continual if you think about it – like visiting another country.'

'Fortuna could be like some weird tourist resort,' said Polly.

Lisa smiled. 'It'll certainly beat Southend.'